*The
Watermelon
Social*

The Watermelon Social

Elaine McCluskey

Gaspereau Press Printers & Publishers 2006

*This book is dedicated to
Andrew, Hannah and Paddy,
who provide love and inspiration.*

Lulu Says She's Sorry
9

Merry Christmas Wherever You Are
25

Queen of the Losers
35

Heart is Here
49

The Watermelon Social
67

The Year of the Horse
83

Strange Girls
97

Moonbeam
111

Eric Montross Sucks
123

One Bad Bounce
133

Lulu Says She's Sorry

I became The World's Strongest Woman thanks to a contrary cow.

On a translucent day in June, the kind of day that makes you turn your face to the heavens like a man released from jail, I was at a 4-H show with my Holstein heifer. The Souris fairgrounds smelled like anxious livestock, and Floss seemed tense. As I drifted, distracted, towards the rabbit hutch, she bolted.

Floss bounded for the highway, me in pursuit. At the edge, near an iron-red bank and a regiment of sentry-straight lupines, I tackled her, and, like a mother who pulls an Olds off a trapped child, hoisted her into the air.

A man stopped his truck. "How much does your calf weigh, miss?"

"Two hundred and eighty pounds," I puffed.

"Do you lift many cows?"

"Not really."

"Would you like to start?"

"I dunno," I answered, noncommittal about most things then.

"I think you'd be good at it."

"All right."

Up to then, I hadn't been good at much. I was an okay 4-H exhibitor, a big girl, which precluded serial dating or cheerleading. After her capture, Floss, an unremarkable black-and-white, placed third. In the ring, I tried to lead her gracefully in a clockwise direction, head high for hubris, moving with the synchronicity of an ice-dancing pair. But it was just okay.

I told my mother about the man in the truck and she phoned.

"I think she has potential," he told my mother, who scrunched her eyes, searching for goblins in the diabolic night.

"Let her go," my father said flatly. "Let her go."

Father was as steady as the Northumberland tide, Mother fanciful, suspicious. Her family was from Ireland, where they believed in changelings and camouflaging boys in flannel dresses lest they end up like Cousin Seamus, replaced by a demented fairy.

The man — his name was Jack Stone — had a powerlifting club in a Quonset barn on his farm. It was a modest set-up: rusty plates, a chalk bowl and bench. Jack wasn't a creep preying on young girls. He was simply a man who liked to see large things moved. He had six lifters, including a boy from my school, a ripped bartender from Charlottetown and an RCMP officer named Svend. "I believe I am descended from the Vikings," boasted Svend. "That's where I get my strength."

Before long, it was clear that Jack was right. I *was* good at something. The genetic gods, the omnipotent beings who made Jimmy Macdonald sharp at algebra and Mary Flanagan a piano virtuoso, had given me juice.

I won provincials my first year, ended up at nationals. I set a dead lift record of four hundred and fifty pounds and spent three years on the power circuit. I felt my muscles shatter like a thin film of ice on a pond, then congeal into a mass, as the air in the gym grew cold and hard and drastic.

My body, too clunky for ballet or cheap cotton clothes from China, finally made sense. Inspired, Jack made T-shirts showing a lifter doing a clean and jerk with gigantic spuds. And then, in a move that seemed as preordained as my serendipitous meeting with Jack, I raised the bar.

I would become, I decided, The World's Strongest Woman.

I'd like to live on a farm with a porch, chickens, goats and cows, a white house with small-paned windows and sleepy rooms that turn, in the afternoon sun, the colour of resin. Spool beds, quilts. I'd like an unfurled driveway anchored by a mailbox, a field of unkempt flowers, wild and surprisingly brittle.

I live in a conundrum of split-levels with vinyl siding, metal doors. Neighbours who call the cops when vagabonds with shopping carts salvage lawn chairs from their trash. The air is so tight, so oxygen-deficient, that you feel as though you are on a transatlantic flight, bombarded by chemicals and pressure, rendered so lightheaded that you snap after the third martini and scream, "Lemmesee the pilot lemmesee the goddamn pilot!"

My husband is a bounty hunter who chases felons to Montreal and Reno. He picked our suburb, close to the U.S. border, for its banality. Why, I ask, since you are never home, do you care where we live? A child of the fifties, he grew up in a time when processed food meant affluence, when developers built houses with incongruous splashes of brick. To this day, he wears his hair floppy, a subconscious testament to his era.

"You look like one of the Monkees," I note dryly.

He smiles, pleased with his floppy hair.

"Now," I add, and then for emphasis: "You look like one of the Monkees *now*."

I like the bustle of the city, the rise and ebb of people, and I like the peace of the country; I just don't like what's in between. It must be me. I see others flourish in suburbs, bonding over yard sales and Whipper Snippers. They walk greyhounds and join golf clubs. They buy competing snow blowers, chainsaws and SUVs, all bigger, more audacious than the last.

*

In winter, the Island hunkered down like a squirrel rat, heartbeat dropping from three hundred to ten times a minute, electrical activities in the brain near undetectable, until the spring, then glorious summer. Flowers bloomed. Students camped on white beaches and thumbed the province, draped, like one-man bands, in pots, packs and acoustic guitars. Nomads slept under lava-red skies and awoke to the cry of gulls, the smell of embers.

I followed my internal blueprint like the birds who fly five thousand miles, navigating with an inner compass and the earth's magnetic field. I felt the burn, developed stretch marks, striations and a power mindset. I tore my left gun, then nursed it back.

"It's in the stars," I believed, like Josephine Blatt who, in 1895, lifted twenty-three men at the Bijou Theatre in Hoboken, New Jersey.

It took me two years to earn the title Josephine once held. Two years of progressive overloads and state fairs, challenges from duds, drunk and sober, who wanted to overpower me in arm wrestling or commando push-up contests.

"We're thinking of bringing in a moose for the lift," a promoter in Timmins once revealed.

"No, I don't think so."

An adult moose can weigh sixteen hundred pounds and looks as awkward as a bobble-headed doll with a massive body and lanky legs.

"How about a grizzly?" he countered, blessed, it appeared, with unlimited access to wild animals.

"Don't they eat people?"

"That's a misconception, actually. They eat their own, mind you, but more people are killed by dogs than by grizzlies. And it's a damn good lift. If we could find one in the fifteen hundred range."

"I think I'll pass."

I specialized in back lifting, which involves a platform containing weights or other objects. Over the decades, those objects have included bull elephants, plates of iron, five-hundred-pound oxen, horses and cavalry men in uniform. I had an aversion to live lifts. I think it's the maternal instinct, protective of life.

In my quest, I appeared in malls, in hockey arenas and on a Toronto radio show with a precious host who feigned befuddlement at my odd avocation. He was a small man with thick glasses and a woollen vest that he wore like an intellectual badge, earned with nicotine stained fingers and an affected pause that suggested that never, in his lofty circle, had he seen anything so rural, so strange.

"Whatwhatwhat is this compulsion?" he stuttered. "And *where* will it end?"

✲

I met my husband when he strode into a Nebraska hospital like Buffalo Bill, handcuffed to a felon named Carlos who was bleeding from the head. The felon, a bail skipper, was wanted for armed robbery and DUI. I liked the fact that Steve was calm with the perilous Carlos, who had one white eye like a poached egg. Before he became a bounty hunter, Steve was a diver who recovered bodies for police. This gave him a peculiar perspective on misery and stress.

We moved to the suburbs after my accident. By the time I had emerged from the fog, by the time my body had stopped crying, we had a vinyl split, a community mailbox and a dead-end street. "It's close to everything," said Steve, which meant the opposite, of course.

I work from home designing web pages. Our closest neighbour is a compulsive lawn mower, a border guard who stones cats and scolds children who step on his grass. His name is Serge. His wife is a despondent pack mule, forced, each weekend, into shifts of redundant lawn work, schlepping fertilizer and seed, growing smaller and muter with each superfluous load.

My husband misses these rituals, camped in towns my daughter and I can never name, chasing cases we can never imagine for fear they materialize, flooding our suburb with rapists, forgers and murderers with plate-sized tattoos of Idi Amin. Gangbangers, toothless crackheads, and perfectly normal-looking people, who, one day, for no apparent reason, steal a child.

"When will he be home?" asks my daughter, knowing my reply.

"I dunno."

*

Last night, while I was sleeping in the tight suburban air, my eye blew up. Not the whole eye, just the white. When I looked in the mirror, past toothpaste and soap stains, I saw a floating blob of blood, as large as a dime, as bright as the poppies back on our farm.

"Yechhhhhhh," shrieked my daughter, shielding her eyes. "It's gross."

It *was* gruesome, the gory red on white, even for someone who had grown up on a farm, someone who had seen a muscle head's tibia snap. It wasn't a gentle streak, the weary pink of bloodshot. It was crimson and it was a message I didn't understand.

What if I had a tumour? A blood clot? I felt vindicated. This was proof, I thought, of how hard it was to breathe under the weight of minivans and cowardly notes stuck in our mailbox accusing us of cinch bugs. My husband phones from Parts Unknown.

I tell him about the notes and my eye.

"You better get it fixed," he says.

"Fixed?"

"You have to take care of yourself; you can't just let yourself get sick."

My last show was in Nebraska, the Cornhusker State, a land of plains and cornfields and astounding clay sculptures carved by the hands of wind and water. Badlands.

The place had an odd quietness, as though the open skies and vast spaces had muffled conversation, dissipated noise. It was hot, and you could feel another force: nature, destiny or maybe the sub-current of Americana. I had slept late and arrived at the fairground minutes before my lift.

At the time, I was dating a steamroller named Willy. Gap-toothed and blond, Willy was an Iowa farmboy, planted among soybeans and corn. His specialty was the two-bucket crucifix, a feat where you stood — Christ-like —

arms outstretched holding buckets filled with cement. Called Wee Willy, he was sweet but one-dimensional, which Willy understood, and I didn't. Willy reminded me of a tomcat we had on the farm, a fat feline named Paddy, who roamed for days and returned with a chewed ear, missing fur, and mice he deposited at my feet with pride.

Willy and I stood in the shade, waiting to follow a ventriloquist named Bert Bodangle, who communicated through an old married couple named Ma and Al, the conveniently drunk husband. I had agreed, against instinct, to do a live lift: a baby elephant named Lulu.

In the wings, I studied Lulu.

"Is she okay?" I wondered.

"Oh yesss," said her trainer, a German named Gunther. "Zisss is a verry vell-trained elephant. She could drive a track-tour."

Lulu looked hot, flapping her ears. Restless. In Asian folklore, elephants are cousins to the clouds and have the power to cause lightning. Lulu was an Asian elephant, born in the grasslands of Sri Lanka, a herbivore with small ears and a dented forehead. She was so magnificent, so overstated, that she had to have a greater purpose, a greater power than *this*.

Elephants are about two hundred and fifty pounds when born and they gain two pounds a day. Still a baby, Lulu weighed fifteen-hundred pounds. I remember counting Lulu's toenails, knowing the larger African elephants have four and trying to remember which was more easily trained, African or Asian.

Led onto my platform, Lulu had a rope around her neck. She was mute, but Gunther had told us that elephants communicate through low-frequency sound waves picked up miles away. Was Lulu calling someone?

The crowd was unsettled, like ducks scattered by a dog. Ma and Al had been ribald but barely funny. I nodded at Willy, offstage in coveralls, and inhaled a gulp of oxygen to my blood. I asked my body to remember the sweat, the burn, the muscle confusion. Just then, I heard a tremendous crack, which could have been lightning, could have been a gun.

Spooked, Lulu lunged. The platform tilted and the crowd shrieked a descending *AAAAaaaaaawwwww* like three thousand Philistines in the temple of Dagon, crushed by the vengeance of a blind, shackled Samson. I tried to compensate, my foot slipped. As I lay on the ground, pinned by my platform and pain so intense that it overwhelmed my senses, sending me to an otherworldly place as enigmatic as the badlands, I heard Gunther calming Lulu. He was speaking in German and in my disconnected state all I could think of was Babylon.

Willy stayed with me and discovered, to his surprise, that he didn't like the smell of hospitals, the decay of flesh. I discovered that Nebraska had an official soft drink: Kool-Aid.

"How's Lulu?" I asked.

"All right," he shrugged. "They gave her bananas, hosed her down."

"That's good."

"She said she's sorry."

✶

We are at a medical clinic, which feels like one of those self-storage units displaced people rent in industrial parks, leaving their most personal belongings behind a blank metal door. The clinic has that rootless air, the air of anonymity and dispassion.

Our doctor has retired, without replacement, so we have become, temporarily, Clinic People. Clinic People drop prescriptions on the sidewalk unfilled; they have health cards from Alberta and cut-off phones. Their visits last as long as a yawn, and they wait hours in a drafty room with posters of rotting lungs. I seat my daughter in a room of hacking children and muttering seniors. On a table is a *Reader's Digest* that smells like Christmas boxes from the attic.

The receptionist looks at no one, just the paper trail. When I complain to my husband about the shabby set-up, he says I'm an ingrate, a right-wing agitator numb to the moral superiority of this country and its mythically friendly folk. "Try living in the States," he says, "where people go *bankrupt* if they get sick!" It's his standard line, his mantra, which I no longer argue.

Name called, I head inside. After a thirty-second examination and two questions, my time with the Clinic Doctor is up.

"Were you hit in the head?"

"No."

"Did you fall?"

"No."

As I feel myself being swept towards the door, I take a stand. Islanders are wary of confrontation, but it's my eye, damn it, and I want more. I wasn't always a Clinic Person. I *was* The World's Strongest Woman. I appeared at the Iowa State Fair, the inspiration for songs and movies, an orgy of Americana, with livestock and orchestras and a celebrated butter sculptor from Toledo who, in 1994, carved a four-hundred-pound likeness of Garth Brooks.

I feel a hand on my back. "Come back if it happens again." The doctor has an accent I place in Romania or the Ukraine. I dig in, plant my feet, bracing for a military press. He pushes harder. Years ago, I would have stored him away as a curiosity, like the man I'd seen riding his bike in a cape and football helmet, but now I am as determined as a pit bull in a *very* small cage.

"Do you know what caused it?"

"No."

Defeated, I leave, passing a man travelling light without shoes or teeth. That night, I think about writing a letter to the editor on social stratification. Or getting an eye patch. I think about how guilty someone will feel when I die of an aneurysm or explosion of the head. I think about telling my husband how I never wanted to live in a lawn-crazed suburb where no one hopes and no one dreams, and everyone drives monstrous SUVs, black hunks of metal and malice, plus-sized symbols of ghetto chic. Funkmaster Flex. The shady mobile. A six-thousand-pound Yukon Denali parked at my curb like a dullahan.

I stop, breathe deeply. "Let's get a kitten," I tell my daughter. "A fat lovey one."

Last year, I went to a strongman reunion in New York.

The room was thick with accents and a subspecies of human: mesomorphs with fast-twitch muscles and thick skin, predisposed to short bursts of energy. Protein guzzlers with a bone structure derived from the mesodermal layer of the embryo. Carnivores with muscles on their digits. I could hear dumbbells crashing to the floor, plates clanking. I could see the skull crusher and smell the burn of lactic acid, as pungent as rubber.

I enjoyed the retrospective honouring Katie Brumbach, a trailblazer born in Vienna in 1884. Katie tossed fourteen-kilogram iron balls into the air and caught them on the back of her neck. She was descended from strong people. My gene was hidden. I was a nine-pound baby who grew to five-nine, one sixty. As a lifter, I added twenty pounds of muscle until my guns reached sixteen inches, my quads twenty-four.

The air had that heaviness big people bring. Most came with sweet dispositions, sowed in childhood. We grew up in an age where hefty children drew praise for their mothers. "Look how sturdy Magnus is. She must be feeding him right." Plump babies were hardy enough to withstand separation or the odd drop to the floor.

My friends had become personal trainers, bodyguards. Bump men. An aspiring actor, Roy Trutka inhabited Gregory the Talking Christmas Tree in a Maryland mall. Roy worked six-hour shifts inside a towering fir with a moving mouth, enduring toddlers and a delinquent who flashed a laser pen in Gregory's eyes.

"Imagine if you had come out of the tree," someone joked.

"Run, you little bastard, run."

Everyone laughed with the generosity of the enormous. I had pictures of my daughter, Lillian, named after a beautiful strongwoman and acrobat, Lillian Leitzel. Born in Germany, Leitzel was only four-foot-nine, and died after falling from rings. My Lillian is strapping; when she was born, Mother placed crosses in her crib to ward off fairies. With the fatalism of the Irish, Mother hated to see anyone too happy, too content, for fear it might all collapse into a mournful mass of howling banshees, unbearable pain.

Bob Baker shredded a telephone book, Ed Patlovski lifted the head table into the air to the tune of "Up Up and Away." It was a night of magnum force.

"You're going to come back," Willy told me. "I know you are."

"I can't," I sighed, pointing at a jagged surgical scar.

"Oh, you'll find a way."

*

I read a story about a cat that lives deep in the African jungle.

The cat has an extra sense. He is able to determine when his prey is sleeping, vulnerable. At that moment, he attacks, ripping the victim to shreds. My neighbour, Serge, is that cat. From his vinyl house, he is able to determine the exact moment that my husband is away and Lillian is sick. Then, he strikes. "Have you noticed anyone rooting through your garbage? We're setting up a neighbourhood garbage watch. We'll need your participation." When I was The World's Strongest Woman, I would have smirked at his world, as tight and compressed as a golf ball; I would have shrugged off the Clinic Doctor and moved on. I had discipline, you see, and superiority, mental and physical, over most people. I was munificent, always, because I felt safe, knowing *they* could never be a threat to me. Why would a woman who deadlifted five hundred pounds, a woman who towed a VW Bug, a woman who trained through a fractured vertebra, care about a man who stayed up all night guarding trash?

These days, I am less magnanimous.

*

Last night, workers were digging up my yard as I waited, filled with dread. Soon, a fat man shouted, "Look, we found it, we've found your baby." Peering into the hole, I saw a newborn with a huge, waxy head. It looked like a zombie baby, and it was *alive*, an omen like my crimson eye. I woke up sobbing.

I hear a door slam, an echo that resonates across the plains of Nebraska. I see a woman who looks like me withdrawing into a cave of conformity where she hides.

I remember my first day at Jack's sweatshop. A breeze was tickling the fields. Up close, Jack was muscular with a head like an ice cream cone, flared from the temples to a curly fro. Svend, the Mountie, was talking about Vikings. "Some warriors were called berserks, you know, and they *were* berserk. They believed that Odin gave them protection and superhuman powers, so they didn't need armour. They'd be so fierce in battle that they would bite their shields. Wounded, they wouldn't feel pain. I'm a bit like that myself."

I nodded at Svend, who had a thunderbolt tattoo. I wasn't about to argue with a Mountie. My father had taught me that. I surveyed the barn, papered with inspirational sayings, including Jack's personal motto: *Lifting is like farming. You got to tear it up to grow*. Svend was still talking about Vikings when I lay on the bench and pressed one sixty five, my very first time. Followed by a clean squat of two sixty.

✳

"Wait until you see what Mommy has."

Lillian is curious, not sure what to expect. With my husband gone, I decide, this is our time to tear it up, to grow. We can buy calico kittens, paint walls amber, plant wildflowers, bright and surprisingly brittle, all with the impunity of The Abandoned. I lift a blanket from the floor, revealing something new, something as magical as butterflies.

"Is that for me?" Lillian asks.

"Yes," I nod. "For you and Mommy."

Last night, as wars waged and spaceships hurtled through the sky, as children learned to walk and merrows seduced sailors, Serge stood outside his house and *glared* at a dandelion on my lawn. Lillian bends to touch the handcrafted barbell, cut down for a ninety-pound frame. The grey metal glistens like a brook teeming with trout; it resonates with the sturdy thickness of a family Bible. It seems so inert, yet filled with latent power, darting neutrons, fissioning force. Lillian lifts it so easily, so naturally, that I laugh out loud.

"When you get bigger, we can add other things."

"Like you used to?"

"Hmmmm, but no elephants."

Merry Christmas Wherever You Are

My husband, a National News Photographer, has just returned from a Federal Election Campaign. (His aggrandizing caps, not mine.)

"Nick was there," he says.

"Nick?"

"You know, Nick Crumb from *The Globe*."

"Oh?" I try to sound blasé.

Crumb is an aging *Globe* photographer, reputed to look exactly like Ernest Hemingway. For years, Crumb, who grew up in public housing in Manchester, has carried this conceit like a letter of reference. The story has grown over the years: during a trip to Cuba, Fidel had singled him out for special treatment because of the eerie resemblance. "Papa, papa," someone claims to have heard Fidel exclaim. For his sixtieth birthday, colleagues gave Crumb a copy of Hemingway's "Letters from Europe." Crumb had shrugged, it was reported, and taken the gift in stride.

"It's true, you know," says my husband, unpacking weeks of dirty socks.

"What?"

"He really does look like Hemingway."

I roll my eyes. Socks are flung across my living room, landing with Crumb-like insouciance. Yes, Crumb is stout with a white beard. Some years back, he started wearing a black beret, claiming neuralgia. When he hit a funk after a back injury, colleagues whispered about a suicide watch. "He doesn't own a gun, does he?" "God, I hope not." Crumb pretended to be nonchalant about the parallels, but occasionally dropped quotes into conversations: "Never mistake motion for action," or his favourite, sage-like: "When people talk, listen completely. Most people never listen."

Crumb's faithful mutt, Blackjack, a gift from the newsroom, became a fixture on his Christmas cards. Crumb and Blackjack camping, Crumb and Blackjack fishing, Crumb and Blackjack in a green canoe. Crumb, the dean of curling photogs, showing Blackjack his cache of lapel pins, his face as bland as a bowl of Reddi-wip.

"I'll show you a better picture," my husband offers. "You'll see."

We drive up behind a local TV news crew tooling about in a four-wheel drive. "Oh, there's the Extra crew," my husband says with a nod meant to look offhand. Offhand. The subtext being *local*: bottom-feeders in the journalistic tank. As we pull out to pass, a suburban family in a GM Suburban, I smile and flash six fingers twice, mouthing: "Channel Six at Six." My daughter laughs and joins in. "Six at Six," we pantomime like Channel Six Newwwwwwwws groupies, overcome by the sight of a real, live newwwwwwws person outside the hokey set.

"Stop it," my husband barks, caught behind a beer truck.
"Mom, someone will see you," whimpers my son.
"Six at six." My daughter convulses with laughter.

I stop my car. Abruptly. Swwiiiiiiisshhh. I hear a wave

mounting, cresting, then breaking under the back seat. For months, my husband denied this phenomenon, stuck to his guns like a UFO-debunker: "Cars don't leak. You must be imagining it." When I finally proved it, showed him the wet floor and gushing seat, he concluded, "You must be leaving the windows open when it rains."

"Huh?"

"You must."

So now after a storm, after rain has poured in through the hatchback and pooled freely under the spare tire, I stop for fun. Swiissssssssssssssh. I get perverse pleasure from this. A validation. Hearing the water mount, crest, then break under the seat, this imaginary water—this clear stigmata—that must be coming in the windows.

"Lift your feet," I yell to the kids. Swiiishhhhhhh.

This time we have stopped for six kamikaze ducks.

Standing among them, arms spread like a messiah, is a man. A wino, a vagrant, dressed by Sally Ann in bell-bottoms and a plaid cotton shirt with snaps. I know they sell those shirts somewhere because I was in Newfoundland once after a Russian trawler sank at sea. When the rescued crew appeared on TV, dazed, displaced, they were all—eight of them—wearing these snap shirts with the row-day-o cut.

This guy looks as if he might have worked on ships, as if he might have had papers and come from Judique or Mabou, as if he might have liked to step dance, to fling his lanky limbs about a linoleum kitchen, before he lost his timing to demons and rum.

Allister, I decide. He looks like an Allister, born to dance on a dime.

As I wait for Allister and his webbed disciples to move, my son eyes the stationary wino.

"Maybe he used to train ducks," he suggests.

"Maybe," I say, not ruling anything out.

My son is four, quiet but observant. As I examine the crude tattoos that extend from under Allister's outstretched sleeve, down to his thumb, an inky road map to a stop too small for eight-hand reels, I realize my son is looking, too.

"I think he might have been in the navy with Poppy."

"Uh huh," I shrug.

This is highly unlikely. Poppy is seventy-nine and got his snarling tiger and purple rose in 1941, during a misbegotten leave in Halifax. Allister, on the other hand, is probably a cruel forty.

Finally, Allister shuffles off. Swwiiiiiiiisshhhhhhhh. We cruise to a stop sign barely fifty metres from the ducks.

"I don't think he was in the navy with Poppy," my daughter pipes up, gloatingly first-born.

Don't start it up, I groan to myself. Don't get it going. But, no, there isn't a fight, an exchange of insults or fists, just a measured discussion of Allister and Poppy and the navy. Poppy was in the navy for six years, 1940 to 1946, six of his forty-five working years, but this is the only job that has registered in their brains, the only way they can see him: sixteen, with slick hair, in a sailor suit, grinning behind a mounted gun. I have explained that Poppy had other jobs — he was a pipefitter and a machinist — but my words are weightless. This was clear last week when I bought a Barrel of Monkeys and packed it for a visit with Poppy.

"Do you think Poppy has played it before?" my daughter asked.

"I think he probably played it in the navy," said my son.

"I don't know," I started to protest, envisioning heavy

seas and circling wolf packs and blood-red curses as a scarlet monkey falls from a chain.

"Think about it, Mom," my daughter upbraided me. "All that time on all those ships."

✳

Two hosers in their twenties are standing outside Zellers, which is abuzz thanks to the release of the long-awaited Club Z catalogue.

"Just a minute, kids." I calm the back seat. I have to watch.

One of the men is short and stocky with a matched set of hoser luggage: a blue kit bag and a two-four. I name him Keith after his favourite brew. Keith has his hands in his pockets and is staring straight ahead, ignoring his buddy, who is agitated and yelling, "I picked you up at the airport, and you said you'd pay me, and now I GOT NO GAS IN MY CAR!!!"

Keith sniffs the air, stares ahead and pretends he cannot hear. He is wearing the full hoser uniform: the ubiquitous leather jacket, jeans and moustache. I imagine they are from Whitney Pier or Gabarus, and have known each other for years. They may be cousins, linked by an illicit spread of hoser genes, and they may not know it.

Jumping and hopping, yelling as though he might cry, the driver slams the hood of his cherry-red Charger and screams, "I GOT NO GAS IN MY CAR!!"

He reminds me of a guy I met in Mabou. He worked on oil rigs and claimed to be a genius. He used "paradigm" and "paradox" and "paranormal" in one breath—a verbal juggler with mad eyes and three psyches in the air. He swore that someday the entire rig would founder, and HE, HE, would save them all.

The driver is still ranting. I wonder how Keith can stay immobile, a master of passive-aggressive torture. A shopper walks by, carrying toilet paper and a dog bed.

"You said you'd—" the crybaby blubbers.

Jesus! The crybaby takes an impotent swing at Keith, who responds with three hard, closed-fist blows to the side of the head. Boom. Boom. Boom. The woman cradles her bed. This isn't Van Damme or Jackie Chan; these aren't stunt doubles with papier mâché props. I can feel the blows. I can hear the sickening crunch of Crybaby's skull, the slap of tearing flesh. Down on both knees, Crybaby holds his head, hands up for protection, while Keith kicks him with a steel-toed boot.

"What's happening, Mom?"

"Ahhhhhh, nothing."

Another kick. Crybaby, broke and injured, is *actually* crying now as he gets into the gas-less car and drives away. Keith, the little prick, sniffs again—one of those don't-look-at-me sniffs—and stares ahead. Untouchable.

I wind down the window of my waterlogged car and yell through the wall of Keith's machismo.

"Cheap creep! You don't even own a car."

*

That night, as my husband checks his email, I re-enact the scene.

"Why do you go to that crummy mall, anyway?" he asks. "There's a crack house nearby, hookers on the corners. I've told you that. The other mall is better."

The other mall is numb and sterile, I want to say. I like it down in the underbelly, rubbing shoulders with the voiceless serfs, the silent majority, standing in line, waiting for a somnambulist clerk to get a price check, to ring through bingo markers and "high pile" animal-print blankets too short for any bed.

When I worked at the newspaper, late at night, when houses were dark, and bars were off-loading drunks, the paper stuffers arrived, one-eyed, crippled, hunchbacked, phlegmy, or so they seemed, emerging from fog and shadows like Jack the Ripper, descending into the bowels of the paper for a few hours, then vanishing into the night. I wait until bedtime, when he starts to complain about a tiff at work. I cut him off, and scream as if I've lost my mind completely. "I got no gas in my CAR! I GOT NO GAS IN MY CAR!"

This, I decide, is my mantra.

I am checking our email: one address, in my husband's name. Since leaving work, I am anonymous, an appendage like Blackjack. I want my own address, free from tips on shooting concerts, free from digital-camera beefs.

A message arrives from Nick Crumb, sent to a brotherhood of photographers across the country. Blackjack's death, and possibly a rise in postal rates, has put Crumb in a reflective mood and he is sending his Christmas greetings through the Net at 2:19 a.m.

Whenever a message from Crumb arrives pinned by a yellow paper clip, I cringe. It is either a photo of Crumb himself caught in a quirky pose, popping up behind Sharon Stone or Hillary Clinton, or a shopworn reminder of Nick's illustrious photo past.

This year, I am not disappointed. As the grainy photo starts to reveal itself on the screen, I see the top of a Charlie Brown Christmas tree being raised to an open sky. Then the words *Merry Christmas Wherever You Are*. Soldiers in some far-flung war, some hellhole of napalm and land mines, are raising the tree against their misery, against the inhumanity of war. Iwo Jima. Mt. Suribachi, volcanic ash mixed with the blood of six thousand martyred Yanks. Christ, I think. Nick is not some washed-up Hemingway pretender without a real life, not some manic-depressive with a dead dog; he's a goddamn war photographer. He's Robert Capa and Joe Rosenthal, Tim Page and the painfully pretty Sean Flynn. Overcome, I want my husband to reply.

"No, leave him alone."
"Please."
"No."
"C'mon."
"The man's dog died."

It is vintage Crumb, so I am intransigent, even with the death of Blackjack. At least, I argue, when a card arrives from Chuck Todd, an unabashed sex offender, a man who travels with inflatable dolls, there is entertainment value: shots of strippers in Santa hats, a fat woman simulating sex with a reindeer. But Crumb is all about Crumb.

I want my husband to take an equally poignant photo, something evocative of his life, his stature. I want him to go to the shopping centre—*my* shopping centre—the one with the dollar store and the day-old bread, the one with duelling hosers, and shoot the regulars scratching their lotto tickets. Maritimers celebrating Christmas despite their misery. Better still, I want my husband mid-pack, scratching the ticket he secretly buys each Friday, and I want the words, forlorn, yet hopeful, *Merry Christmas Wherever You Are* drifting off the page.

*

My husband is gone. It's been three weeks since he left for Sweden (to cover curling), two weeks since my son developed bronchitis, and I found a rat in the upstairs toilet. One ugly, pointy-headed beast that I murdered with a fury that surprised me.

> To: Sixnews@ns.sympatico.ca
> CC: leica@istar.ca
> Subject: Channel Six at Six
>
> Dear Mary and Geoff,
>   I love your show, particularly when Mary wears the green suit that matches her eyes. Your story on grieving for pets (Hammy's Heartbreak) really struck a chord. As Mary so eloquently put it: *pets are people, too*. Since when is the value of a life determined by your number of toes? Since when is sorrow furless?
>   Thank you Six at Six for telling it like it is.
>   Ciao
> An avid fan

Queen of the Losers

Phyllis stops at table three, occupied by six women, one conspicuous in a floor-length white gown with stand-up collar.

The gown looks like something from the Grand Ole Opry with a cinched waist and lace trim, hand-sewn for a bluegrass legend, an old doll with a mountain whang and a guitar. The woman appears thirty-five, with a David Bowie shag. Taking a resolute breath, she leans forward and blows out the sparklers on the cake that Phyllis has ceremoniously delivered. Queen of the Losers 2004.

The ladies-in-waiting clap; the queen sighs in her too-tight gown. For a glorious monarch in a sash and crown, for a celebrated loser in a rooster cut, she looks unmistakably sad. Under the tipsy grins and name tags, so do most of the others.

The room is thick with the smell of fried fish and one hundred women, linked by carbs and trans fats, a collective will to shed. They have driven across the county in Dodge pickups and spunky Ford Festivas. Bottle blondes and haggard brunettes, housewives, school-bus drivers, farmers, all with titanic hips and rubber bellies. Their faces have been shaped by disappointment and now, in a weekend of forced frivolity, they are trying to forget.

"To our queen, Denise, who lost thirty-six pounds." Applause for the queen, who has circles under her eyes like gravy stains. "You are inspiration to all Eat to Live members."

They clap and return to their food. In a tacit agreement, sealed with the first donair, the dietary gates have been opened to deep-fried ice cream, cheesecake and oceans of Baby Duck. Chicken wings stand in line behind greasy bruschetta. Mounds of boiled carrots and turnips, the mandatory complement to every entree, have been shoved aside in slag heaps.

Phyllis, a pro after eighteen years, clears the queen's table first. "Would you like anything else?" she asks, deferential.

"No," says the queen demurely, pushing aside a stack of rib bones.

The Bright Spot Motel boasts a full menu and the only conference room for miles. The room is located in the basement, near laundry and a twelve-metre pool, ensuring that meetings are steamed in bleach and chlorine. Other selling points: free cable, sports rates for teams, pet access and non-smoking rooms that reek of Export A. Phyllis marches to the back, where one woman is fading into the maroon walls, dark enough to cover stains and culinary misadventures, accented with inconceivable florals and pictures of dogs.

"You're doing a lovely job," offers the woman. She is seated under a dog in a fire hat, part of the curious motif that has branded the washroom doors Pointers and Setters.

"Why thank you. I've been at it for a long time."

"Well, you're a professional. My name is Fern."

Fern has blonde hair in a French twist, turquoise eyes that sparkle like Austrian crystals. Her huge body is encased in a caftan that moves, she imagines, with the panache and abandon of Stevie Nicks.

"I'm Phyllis."

"Have you ever been south, Phyllis?"

"No, but I'm going to go someday."

After two decades of humping plates, Phyllis is thin and gnarled as a walking stick. Under five feet, she drives a Geo Metro with a cushion on the seat. Her husband pilots a beige '79 Dodge shortbox with one black door.

"I went one winter and could have stayed forever," Fern sighs, exhaling a rush of warm nights and bawdy bougainvilleas. "When I hit that beach, I *knew* I was home. I closed my eyes and imagined the sun was melting the fat under my skin, like a roasting chicken. After an hour, I knew I was baking, and the fat was seeping out, dripping down my sides onto the sand. Yellow and clear."

"That's it," swears Phyllis, as though she's been sold. "I *have* to go."

When Katrina was a toddler, Fern would take her to the Shore Mall, a six-store complex with a coin-operated squirrel outside Bob's Hardware.

Near the chipped squirrel was a photo booth that offered four poses for three dollars. The Formica booth was rundown but mystical as a fortune teller with a half curtain and a seat that bored kids spun round on until they toppled off. Outside were samples under Plexiglas. The models appeared to be from Boston or California, Fern determined, with tans and button-down collars, all except for one man, added for diversity, in a cowboy hat.

"Wait here, dear," she whispered one day.

Fern pulled the curtain, exhilarated by the modest indulgence. She changed the background from orange to navy. Who could wear orange? In private, she sucked in her cheeks. Her face seemed thinner, she concluded, haughty like Sharon Stone, like someone who knew her way around life.

Click. Click. Click. Click.

Fern waited. Four minutes. Maybe it took longer in The County, the city name for dots on the Maritime map, a smattering of houses, a gas pump and a Quick Stop. Boarded-up dairy bars. In The County, seniors dressed up on Sundays and drove to a restaurant where the plastic menus never changed, where no one noticed shelves of rubber gloves and batteries near your table, or the pump attendant who ducked inside for change. Crib games were Wednesday at the legion. In New York, Fern had heard, hip people played sardonic games in photo booths. They donned horns and held up signs, one per frame: Will Sing For Dough. Fern heard a grinding noise like a garburator.

She looked inside the metal chute. Nothing.

"Mom?"

"Just a couple more minutes."

Fern studied a bulletin board: *Woodstove, guaranteed to heat all night. Fertilizer spreader, 400-pound capacity.* Another grinding of gears, then predictably, disappointingly, nothing.

Katrina in tow, Fern drove home. The next week, she returned to the mall and found herself drawn to the photo booth. Good Lord. There it was. The price of vanity, the charge for self-indulgence: her pictures, a strip of grinning, vamping poses posted for everyone to see, under Plexiglas, next to the man in the cowboy hat, who *had* to be an actor.

∗

The motel window is jammed with an air conditioner that's missing dials. Shivering, Fern tosses under a synthetic bedspread that feels like fibreglass, too stiff to wrap around her body, too brittle for comfort. She tries to ignore the light creeping under the door, blocked unsuccessfully with a rolled-up towel. She wishes the weekend was over.

Fern thinks about the time her mother opened the newspaper to a photo taken in the Public Gardens in Halifax, an idyllic vignette of romance and youth. In the picture, a girl was admiring tulips under the wing of an American sailor in whites. Fern remembers staring at the unmistakable black bangs and jutting jaw of her classmate, Eileen Smeltzer, a poor girl from a shack down the road, then at her mother's disapproving face. Did the paper know Eileen was twelve? Did the sailor?

Outside Fern's door, in a tunnel of smoke and pizza vapours, two losers are propped up. Unable to sleep, Fern listens but breathes softly to avoid detection. Velma, a bookkeeper, is flaunting her new status. It is well known (thanks to Velma) that her daughter Jacki is living with a sixty-year-old doctor. Jacki has ditched her second husband and kids and moved in with the physician.

"She just wants to be happy," says Velma, puffed with pride.

"What's wrong with that?" concurs Bernice, who has dropped twelve pounds, putting her in the mood to humour Velma.

"She's pretty sure she's going to get a ring."

"That would be nice."

"Oh yes."

"Is he still drinking so heavy?" asks Bernice, who has grey hair, as coarse as bear fur, and a necklace honouring Dale Earnhardt's Number Three.

"Nooooooo," Velma scoffs, raising her voice for eavesdroppers like Fern. "He *never* had a drinking problem, that was just jealous people talking. They see an intelligent man with money."

"They're all the same, the bastards."

"He has a place in Florida, you know, he says I can stay anytime."

"That's wonderful, ain't it?"

"Hmmmm."

"And he got his licence back?"

"Oh yes, ages ago."

*

When Fern went south, it was, quite improbably, to Club Med.

She had never been past Moncton, a fact she kept to herself when she shuffled into Gail's Travel and Gail confided, "This is very popular." Sounding worldly, as though she was tired of the French Riviera or West Palm Beach, Fern shrugged. "Time for something different."

The resort was Porta something or other, not far from Venezuela, if you looked on a map. Meeting her on the runway, the heat was so intense that it knocked the breath from Fern's chest. Vacationers piled onto a bus that careened down unlit streets, around corners, clinging to cliffs. At the resort, they were given bracelets and shown their tiny rooms. "Don't worry," the greeter told Fern. "No one spends much time here." Fern's roommate was from Martha's Vineyard, a freckled divorcee who ran a flower shop. Kate was in her second week, already immersed in nude body painting, talent shows and kitchen help.

Fern took a tour of a waterfall in the jungle, swam in a lagoon.

She met a couple from Etobicoke, on the lam from their respective spouses. At the far end of the beach, she caught glimpses of blasé Germans strolling naked. One night, Fern ended up at an outdoor bar with two guests and a staffer named Phillippe from France. He was trying to dazzle a Japanese woman, a pharmacist from New York, while Fern and a senior named Woody filled out the table.

"Let us tell our most outrageous sexual experience," Phillippe proposed daringly.

The pharmacist giggled; Phillippe sat back and waited like a vulture.

"Woody, you go first."

Woody, a widower, told something about a maid in Paris during the war. Fern was impressed, but stuck. She had had only two dates in her life, both uneventful. Her mind flashed to a February day when she was in Halifax for a doctor's appointment, and, short on bus fare, walked the bridge. It was cold enough to sting your lungs, and cars were racing through mounds of slush, assailing her. Fern hated heights, and on a bridge like this, jumpers could go at any second, wretches driven too far by slush and defeat and numbing isolation.

"I had sex on the Angus L. Macdonald Bridge with a stranger," she blurted.

Phillippe nodded approvingly.

"What is the Angus L?" the pharmacist asked.

"Kinda like the Golden Gate."

"Ahh," she nodded.

"I saw this man coming from the opposite direction and something clicked."

"You did it there?" asked Phillippe, who seemed, to Fern, too cozy with Ted, the tennis instructor.

"Yeah."

"Did you ever see him again?"
"No."
"Ahhh," they said, relinquishing the floor to Eko, the pharmacist, who picked up with, "Once, when I was at my health club...."

*

Fern cracks her door and peeks into the hall, littered with a KFC bucket, chicken bones and two drained Pepsis. Bernice had tired of Velma's gloating and retired, leaving the night to drunker, meaner losers.

"You can kiss my ass."

"I couldn't miss it."

No longer in her Opry dress, the queen is bickering with a trucker named Ralph who is clasping a bottle of moonshine like a Bible. Ralph, who has emerged from nowhere, is five-foot-three with spittle on the corners of his beard. Sweat-stained, he looks like a deranged leprechaun in a cowboy hat and leather vest, under which he is shirtless. The queen has changed into a T-shirt that claims, "I'm too sexy for my hair."

"You bastard," she curses.

"You know I don't mean that, sweetheart. It's a damn fine ass."

Outside Fern's room, the convention has descended into defiant boozing, lewd jokes and flashes of irrational anger. The air feels like an election-night party upended by defeat, saddled with regrets and recriminations. All around her, Fern can see Eat to Live pounds creeping back like black mould, a micro-organism of dormant spores that cannot be stopped. Where were the seminars, the motivational speakers? Pilates?

"I'm a drunken man on a Halifax pier ..." Down the

hall, a guitar leads a sodden singalong into its fifth hour. Through her cracked door, Fern watches Ralph and the queen grope their way into the Eat to Live party room. She hears a window open, a bottle smash, a collective cackle, then silence. Fern sees a mean streak in the queen, like the relatives of rapists you watch in court, heckling victims with taunts like "It sucks to be you." The elevator parts for an exasperated woman in pyjama pants, the same woman Fern had seen arriving earlier in a Chevy Trail-Blazer with kids. The woman, wearing a New York Marathon T-shirt, glares at Fern with contempt.

"You should be ashamed of yourselves," she spits. "There are children trying to sleep."

"But I ..."

Fern looks at her accuser. She is skinny with hollow eyes that are chasing something elusive, something that manicures and marathons can never yield: validation, or consolation for being small and plain and quite unlovely.

"I called security three times and they say they won't do anything because *you people* have half the hotel booked."

"I'm not...."

"No wonder you're so fat."

*

Of course, there was no stranger on the bridge. But there was, a year later, a Russian sailor named Ivan. It was during the Tall Ships visit of 1984 and Halifax was drunk on uniforms, accents and towering ships with mysterious origins. It was like wartime again. Fern had read a story about an African tribe on a remote jungle island. If a ferry boat passed, tribesmen went mad, wading past man-eating crocodiles, waving, shouting, excited to see something new. Halifax was that island.

The city was hot when seventeen hundred sailors, mainly cadets with an exotic whiff, arrived. The ships were feted, celebrated. Girls trotted out for a dance at the Metro Centre. Downtown were jugglers, mimes and magicians. When you went to the mall, you saw sailors with aging desperadoes and underage girls like Eileen, the same girls who met the U.S. destroyers with open arms and dreams of moving to Carolina. After a week of debauchery, cynics dubbed the finale, the glorious Parade of Sail, the Parade of Tail. People clapped when a crewman from an Italian ship tossed a girl his blue hat.

"Come back," she shouted through tears.

"I will."

Fern went back home and stayed, but sometimes she dreamed. She saw four masts towering over the grain elevator, she saw a sailor climb the booms to secure a sand-coloured sail. She rented *Dr. Zhivago*, she read *War and Peace*. She rewatched *Reds* and she became an expert on the last czar, Nicholas II, and the gruesome execution of his family in a Yekaterinburg cellar. Fascinated by Rasputin, the mad monk, she imagined, without much trouble, that her town was a remote Siberian village, buried in snow and mud and desolation. And then, a few years ago, Russians opened a corner store in Dartmouth selling hockey cards, pop and novelties. She went inside, looking for something she never found.

*

It's seven a.m. and the pool deck is empty. Two unfamiliar men arrive, crisp and ironed as bank notes. The older man, bald and smelling of money, is wearing a white robe; his companion is in Elvis Costello glasses.

After Katrina was born, Fern opened a hair salon and gradually outgrew her clothes, driven to eat by overpowering urges she couldn't explain. Was it boredom, restlessness, some bid to extirpate her former self? It was like the tattooed woman she had seen on TV. The behaviour had started innocuously, the woman explained, with a shamrock on her hip. "I had no intention of getting my whole body done, but I just found myself adding." Fern had had no intention of reaching two hundred and sixty pounds, of being so large that she wore sleeveless shifts in winter, sandals in snow.

Fern stares across the deck.

The older man crawls on rundown batteries. He has dead, decision-making eyes that do not flicker, eyes that have seen too much to be frightened by his new drained state. Elvis buzzes at his side.

When Fern was at Club Med, a green schooner anchored one night in the moonlight like an apparition. From her room, she watched two men row ashore: one, she later discovered, was a mogul from Virginia, the other, a hired hand named Jack.

Kate set her sights on Jack and Fern ended up at the bar talking to the mogul, who had once sailed to Nova Scotia. His name was Chip—she had never met a Chip—and he was divorced. He'd been a Navy SEAL in Vietnam before investing in software.

Fern watches the older man wade into the pool where he launches into a feeble breaststroke, barely moving. Suspended in gel, he stares at the end of the pool, appearing to see nothing while Fern knows he sees it all.

"Come on, come on." Elvis follows him, waving his arms, as though he is flagging down a rescue plane. "Come on."

The swimmer continues, chin skimming the surface, legs dangling. It is so much effort that it reminds Fern of a child wading through towering snowdrifts to school.

Finished, the man climbs out, drained but impassive in tailored trunks. Elvis dashes over and grabs his shoulder, oozing, "This is your best day yet. You're a machine, you're a machine."

The lizard eyes are flat as the man retrieves his towel, crosses the deck and stops at Fern. He looks at her as if she deserves an explanation, as if she is the kind of woman who understands the way life works. Fern thinks about sunshine, about a moonlit bar. Before Chip had returned to his schooner, he'd brushed a blonde hair from Fern's tanned face and whispered, without shame or compunction, with the poise of a man who'd once wielded a crossbow, "You have the most beautiful breasts." In the hedonistic moment, coloured by heat and lust and an all-inclusive bracelet, you were free to be who you were or who you wanted to be.

She meets the lizard eyes.

"All my life, I was terrified of the water. When my wife was alive, I wouldn't go on a cruise, I wouldn't go fishing." He says the words with import, as though he had discovered a profound truth. "Now, I have a Belgian fellow teaching me back in Montreal. The first lesson, he threw me in the deep end. Sometimes, that's what it takes."

Fern nods, knowing the price of shame, the cost of trepidation. Elvis rushes up and grabs the older man's elbow. "He's doing great. Just to see him in there."

"He's my assistant," the man explains, keeping his eyes on Fern. He shuffles off, towel around him, weightier matters to deal with, while the younger man, all bounce and exuberance, follows.

*

Fern blows a mental kiss to Katrina, now off at college. She thinks about heat and the smell of bougainvilleas. On the Internet recently, she stumbled upon a website with photos of naked middle-aged people at a resort. Loose and flabby as elephants' skin, they had surgery scars and stretch marks and penises that barely poked through folds of fat, little round bulbs of manhood. Naturists. The women had deflated breasts and they faced the camera joyfully, unconcerned, it seemed, by cellulite or the ravages of time, finding liberation in their repugnant skin. At some point, Fern decides, you have to forgive yourself—for everything. Every mistake, every weakness, real and imagined.

"You bastard." The queen staggers onto the deck pursued by Ralph. Fern recognizes him now as a Goodey from Turk's Harbour. For years, the Goodeys had been embroiled in a feud with the Crooks. The Crooks, well, the Crooks lived up to their name. They'd burn your shed, poison your dog, strip the wheels off your pickup. No one remembered how the feud started, but it lasted for years, and carried on to the St. Joseph's graveyard, where Mrs. Goodey buried her husband with one last shot:

Here lies Alonzo Goodey driven to his death by the non-stop aggravation of Sherman Crook and his no-good thieving sons. May they burn in Hell.

Sherman lasted only two years after Alonzo; there wasn't much to live for with Alonzo gone.

Ralph and the queen scuffle; she lands in the pool with a curse. When she surfaces, her Opry gown is see-through, her rooster cut wasted. Turning towards the entrance, Fern spies the blonde woman from the hallway, still thin, still unlovely, shaking her head at the tawdry spectacle. Fern cocks her chin at a haughty angle. She moves her chair across the deck under a window where a single ray of sunlight hits her blonde hair and her beautiful travelled bosom.

Heart is Here

Through the open door, I could see Dr. Miller with a patient, who was flopped in a chair like a hand puppet, toothless and slack. She might have been sixty-five or ninety, struggling to breathe.

Patrician, Dr. Miller was a soap opera doctor with a leather bag and stethoscope. Over eighty, his hair was ivory, skin draped over scrupulous bones like sheets over fine antiques. Dr. Miller stared at the woman for an interminable thirty seconds, at her shabby clothes and greasy hair, at her wanton past and woebegone ways, until she blinked.

"Go home, you're through!" he ordered. "You wasted this life. Make a better stab at the next."

"But …" protested the woman, reeling. She had a fighter's nose sunk into a broad face, dull and sooty from living in the shadows. On the ropes, she sucked in air. *Nnnnhhh-hhhhh.*

"No bellyaching," barked Miller. "Where would I be today if I had been a bellyacher?" He plowed on, a one-man wrecking crew emboldened by age and rank and dementia. "I'd still be in France with Krauts chasing me down like hounds after a fox, and say what you will about the Krauts, they were expert marksmen."

I turned away, scanning the room, one corner of a three-storey building. On a table sat a jigsaw puzzle, a

German castle set in mawkish mountains, drawbridge missing. Copies of *Chatelaine* with ancient Christmas recipes involving marshmallows.

*

Dot, the zombie receptionist, had a lineup from the door to her white enamel desk. She had files on the carpet, files in milk crates, files spilling from a glass cabinet like lava: appendectomies, CAT scans, psychiatric evaluations, lower intestine complaints laid bare.

Dr. Austin Miller is retiring. Patients of Dr. Miller may pick up their files Friday from 2 p.m. to 4 p.m. at his Pier St. office.

"Name?" Like an automaton, Dot addressed a vagrant who wasn't wearing shoes, just work socks decorated with road salt that glistened. He probably came from a town of closed mines and dead dreams, numbed by drugs from the Alberta oil fields.

"Raymond mmmmmmm," he muttered, a potpourri of mouthwash and mould.

"Do you have any ID, Raymond?" Dot ignored his shoeless state. Raymond's T-shirt, recycled from the street, promised *Success Without College* over the faces of unschooled celebrities, mostly rappers, mostly dead.

"Mmmmmm."

"Driver's licence?"

"Mmmmmmmm."

"SIN card?"

"Mmmmm."

"Just sign here." Dot pulled a file from a crate marked Alives, next to the Deads.

She shoved it forward like a bus ticket. I recalled the U.S. debate over the sanctity of medical records, with Bill

Clinton warning Americans to safeguard their credit and employment reords, but this was Nova Scotia not D.C. As Raymond wafted away, a teen in Nancy Sinatra knee-high boots teetered in with a baby. I tried to match the baby with one of the lopsided pictures on Dr. Miller's bulletin board, but they were all Jerry Springer babies with pierced ears and lace headbands, all named Charitee and Deneeze.

File in hand, I passed a barred drugstore, dodging gangstas in Speedo hologram goggles with snake eyes. Once blue, the edge of my file was frayed. Dr. Miller eschewed technology, affecting a crusty New England asceticism as though he belonged in a movie with Katherine Hepburn. I opened the cover gently, touching the blood and fibre of my life.

> Jane Hawes
> AGE: 28 Years   D.O.B. 75-04-16
> UNIT NO. 870
> PHYSICIAN: Miller
> ACCESSION NO: S99-4689
> SEX F
> QWARD GMH
> ACCESSION DATE: June 22
> SPECIMEN: Placenta
> GROSS: The specimen is a singleton placenta. Weight and measurements are:
> CORD: 29.0 cm
> CORD INSERTION FROM MARGIN: central, 7.0 cm
> MEMBRANE RUPTURE FROM DISC MARGIN: 2.0 cm
> DIMENSIONS: 20.0 × 15.0 cm
> WEIGHT: 540 gm
> ABNORMALITIES: None
> ESTIMATED FETAL WEIGHT: 1886 grams -/+ 377 grams.

Who, I wondered, is Jane Hawes? Why were her records in my file? I am Walter Sparrow, professor of history, husband of Beatrice Bambury. I was born in the North End of Halifax in 1953, and at one point, with the arrogance of youth, called myself a citizen of the world, a sovereign creature in the Sartre mould.

Curious, I shuffled through Miller's notes, which were elegantly written, belying the fact that, despite his fine looks and pedigree, he was the doctor of last resort. All the new doctors, the ones with computer records and kids in private schools, were full.

Juggling my file on my lap, I drove past a taxi stand manned by Russians, burly enigmas with ponytails and murky pasts. I pulled onto Main Street ahead of a Jimmy driven by a dude in a ball cap. He looked like a guy who played old-timers' hockey at three a.m., drinking beer and dropping stone cold dead on a rush to the net. Instead of maintaining speed, he performed the patented hoser manoeuvre, accelerating until he grazed my bumper and beeeeeeeppped.

In my file was a letter from an allergist. During my visit, Dr. Quinton J. Mallard had worked through a series of queries about carpeting, insulation, heating, forcing me to lie when I didn't know the answers. He felt my adenoids, measured my skull, then stared into my eyes and asked, "Do you and your wife enjoy a healthy sex life?"

I examined a report from the hospital that treated me after a car crash. The x-ray technician had been a sprite named Pat who was into winter surfing, clean, with buffed nails and lemony hair, so precise she could have been outlined with a Japanese brush dipped in ink.

I read down. Rib bruising, no fracture.

Situs inversus totalis. I blinked. I held the paper close as the hoser honked again.

What the hell is this?

Situs inversus totalis. I pulled over. Oh God, it sounded serious.

Immediately, I recalled a story about a college basketball player who learned, at age twenty, that he had Marfan syndrome, a form of gigantism. He died from complications. I am only five foot ten but this could *still* be something awful, a genetic time bomb. Given my family's predilection for half-truths and secrets, I'd never know. My father didn't tell us Aunt Gertie was dead until we went to Mass and the priest offered prayers for her soul. Oh God.

Situs inversus totalis
There it was on the Internet.

> Mirror image of the organs
> In the United States, *Situs inversus* occurs in 0.01% of the population.
> MORTALITY/MORBIDITY: Typically, patients with *Situs inversus* have a normal life expectancy. In the rare cases of cardiac anomalies, life expectancy is reduced. Patients with Kartagener syndrome have a normal life expectancy if the bronchiectasis is treated adequately.
> RACE: No racial predilection known.
> SEX: The male-to-female ratio is 1:1.
> AGE: *Situs* abnormalities are congenital.

Good God! I screamed. My heart, liver and spleen are on the wrong side of my body. I am a freak, the flip side of normal.

I vowed not to tell Beatrice, a writer. I would not, I decided, give her evidence of my peculiarities, fodder for a pathetic character. I could see it in print: jokes about heart attacks. Will the pain shoot up his right arm or left? Should he get a locator tattoo: Heart Is Here? I cursed the whiners who appeared on Oprah, traumatized by an unknown sibling or a jailed relation. How would they deal with this: total reversal of the organs?

*

BEATRICE'S NOTEBOOK:

Last night, Walter complimented me on my hair. His flattery is well-meaning but suspect. After we met, during the months of passion and possibilities, Walter gushed, "Wait until you meet Bernie. Bernie will really like you." This, I was led to believe, was the litmus test.

We went to the North End where my husband had grown up near an abattoir and where Bernie still resided. In a dingy restaurant with chrome chairs surrounded by gravy vats and a sign: Washroom for Customers Only, we met Bernie. It was two p.m. Bernie was on a disability pension. He lived with his mother in the same apartment they had inhabited since 1967 and he rebuilt guns, under the table, for pocket money.

Twice, Bernie's friend, Cyril, stumbled to the washroom to hurl, making me feel like I was trapped in a Diane Arbus photo. Walter gave all his old friends the same extravagant buildup. When I met them, I was shocked to see potheads, psychiatric patients, the chronically unemployed. He romanticized them all, saw something in them that didn't—to my mind— exist, all of which made me question myself. If his judgment was this skewed, his lens this blurred, what did it say about me? Beatrice.

*

Still reeling, I settle down long enough to check my email.

> TO: Professor Sparrow
> FROM: Adam
>
> I am sorry I cannot complete my assignment. I have been unable to concentrate due to the war in Afghanistan and Kobe Bryant's trial. I feel like I am sinking in a sea of irrelevance. Your humble student and ardent admirer,
>   Adam.

Hitting delete, I dismiss Adam, who does not deserve my attention at a time like this, consumed as I am with *situs solitus*, ciliary dyskinesia and the capricious way an embryonic heart can make a fateful loop to right instead of left. I skim an Internet study with mice; I muddle through genetic mutation, Gregor Mendel and DNA nucleotides, but it's just too much.

There is also an email from Sarah, who at twenty-five has the edge of being older, travelled. In the same way I ration beer, I try not to call on her too often in class, but her answers are so earnest, so self-effacing. She tilts her head sideways with a smile I try to ignore, but secretly await each class.

✶

I head to the Y to try out my organs.

At the entrance, I pass Bim, a regular who drives a beer truck and sweats serenity. Bim walks on his toes, a springy walk, unmenacing, free of machismo. He opens the door for seniors, and swings a kit bag like a WW II sailor on shore leave.

Bim says hello and I feel better.

After twenty laps in the pool, nothing seems amiss. I touch my heart repeatedly like someone with a new haircut. I try to ignore the shallow end, churning with old women tossed about like driftwood, led by an aqua-fitness instructor who kicks the air to the Dixie Chicks. In this grey sea, in a pallid singlet, is a lone man with a moustache and glasses. Why is he here? Was he injured in a car crash? Does he lust after the instructor? His uninhabited face tells me nothing.

I believe in karma so I think of doing something selfless. In the dressing room, I spot Robbie, a slow-witted kid lost in a world of Pokemon and cosmic warriors. "Nice day, isn't it, Robbie?" I offer through a gauzy veil of understanding.

Robbie lurches forward and I flinch. Does he realize I avoid him? Does he care? Robbie leans so close I can count the freckles on his nose, see the vacuum behind his eyes. "Do you know what really scares me?" Is Robbie, the dolt who tips the vending machines for change, the sad sack who carries Skoal cherry dip in a fanny pack, about to confide in me? I flinch again. "When I'm watching a horror movie." He stares, face cocked sideways like a loaded pistol. "And the person being chased has the same first name as me."

*

"What do you believe prompted the Volstead Act?" I call on a chubby girl, who stammers, eyeing the floor, chin tucked inward as though she's warding off a blow. I rock on my heels and nod profoundly. "That's very insightful."

"Sarah?" Is she wearing a Sailor Moon t-shirt? As Sarah discusses American mores in the twenties, I notice Adam playing Tony Hawk's Pro Skater 4 on his laptop. My course is called "Prohibition: The Impact on Atlantic Canada," and we look at rum-runners and coast guard raids and speakeasies. It is usually full, not as popular as Modern American Culture, which dabbles in LSD, CB radios and Archie Bunker, but still, I believe, appealing.

Back in my office, I am confused by Adam, whose mother has twice visited, brandishing a medical letter. I wonder if Adam is failing in order to defy her, to repudiate her life. I grew up in a prefab with two bedrooms and a console TV in the living room. Despite our modest circumstances, my father believed he was oozing with charm, an irascible scoundrel who could bark with impunity, "Will someone muzzle that baby?" or "When will broads learn their place?" Of course, no one was charmed. Not by this minor man who had never done anything dashing or bold. He had no licence for the outrageous; he hadn't written a great book or rubbed out an enemy line in France. He wore polyester pants, opal or green, winched to a self-induced wedgie. A plumber for thirty-eight years, my father never missed a day of work, but people didn't care. They would bite their collective tongues and hate HER. Her obsequiousness, her piety, the way she clasped an illusory rosary, always rubbing, stained with sin. If she'd had more class, less baggage, he wouldn't have felt superior based solely on a bell curve of two. I believe my mother, sin-stained and simple, thought we were destitute, that she didn't know my father ran a steady tab at the Gentleman's Club, gambling on the charms of a redheaded floozy named Dee.

Sarah's paper, a look at smuggling on Saint Pierre and Miquelon, is well done, but not remarkable. It's not as good as Nate's, but Nate's genius is locked in a battle with madness and drugs so he can't be counted on. When Nate skips class, he concocts elaborate fantasies about grisly deaths and imaginary girlfriends. I would like to give Nate and Sarah both an A, but it would be a stretch.

I wonder what Sarah got last term from Sneddon, who has given the same lectures for eight years. Sneddon's indolence comes from the fact that he is consumed with his hobby, "listening to music." Sneddon has thousands of CDS, which, with a straight face, he describes as "an eclectic mix of pop and country." Jimmy Buffett, AC/DC, Randy Travis, and, for intellectual punch, Bruce Cockburn. His collection resides in a room dominated by phallic speakers on the monumental scale of a Henry Moore sculpture, alive, expansive, magnetically shielded to prevent interference with the big-screen TV.

Sneddon is charged with teaching "Changes in Nova Scotia Social Structure in the 1800s," but, somehow, has shifted the entire focus to two Nova Scotia giants born in the 1800s. Angus McAskill, immortalized on Citadel Hill with a life-size likeness, was seven foot nine. Anna Swan, an eighteen-pound baby, became the tallest woman in the world. She performed for P.T. Barnum and married another giant in a spectacular wedding.

Entering the hallway, I hear students grumbling.

They freeze. Cast as an interloper, I am mildly offended. "Go ahead," I smile, recalling the conviction of my youth, a time of peace rallies and protests. In grad school, in a lapse I am embarrassed to admit, I belonged to a group obsessed with the Zazous of Vichy France, rebellious youth inspired by jazz and swing, defying the conservative styles of the Nazis. We wore belted zoot suits, long greasy hair and brightly coloured socks, until it all became too much. I lived in a bare room with a mattress, but the space was filled with rhetoric and liberal thought.

"Don't let me interrupt."

The grumbling resumes.

"Well, I think they should kill them all starting with Old Man Bush, then W."

"Yeah," a boy in spiked hair agrees.

"Spare the twins?" asks a girl.

"Yeah, but kill all the other despots in the world."

"What about Laura?" she wonders.

"Smoke her too."

BEATRICE'S NOTEBOOK:

Last night, Walter ran me a bath, lighting an arc of candles around the tub. It is penance, I assume, for buying a pair of ridiculous sunglasses at that outdoor store he frequents.

"They look really silly," I offered.

"They're glacier glasses," Walter protested.

"Glacier glasses in Halifax?"

"Fine, I will take them back. There is nothing wrong with good eyewear but I will take them back. If you want to ruin your eyes with cheap glasses...."

I am not sure if the glasses went back but Walter did make a special effort. I heard a curse when he put a match to a mousse can, which he had mistaken for a candle. "You have to get real glasses," I urged.

Yesterday, I bought glasses of my own. Afterwards, I could read but it was as though someone had opened the drapes, exposing the furniture as dusty and worn. In the hyper-lit mall, I looked shabby, and all around me were crisp hairdos and waxed brows. My highlights were orange not gold, and, to my horror, I could see a stain on my pants. When had people abandoned blue leather jackets? When had earflaps come back? I was the man in the mullet, the woman in the poodle perm; I was the bumpkin who carried his car stereo by the handle into stores, lest it be lifted. And thongs? Why, in God's name, were the stores filled with thongs?

Walter seems strange, as though he's hiding something. Beatrice.

*

Sarah's chair is under a pot light, caught in an interplay of light and shade, and she is talking to Adam. Her boyfriend met her at the Tokyo airport, she says, and they got on a commuter train crammed with travellers and yakuza tattoos. Adam's back stiffens, his hands clutch his text, and I know he is thinking, "She's had sex."

Her father, an architect, had become obsessed with minkas, centuries-old farmhouses in the hills of Japan. As she describes sleeping Japanese style on the floor of their resurrected minka under dark beams and smoke-stained posts, Adam's face twitches.

"After that, I went to UBC for a while but I wasn't sure what I wanted," she admits. "I wasn't a brilliant student, I started hanging with a rough crowd. I needed to leave my hometown." And Adam thinks, "Oh my God, she's been with a rough crowd, she's had sex."

Every clue leads in one direction: she owns a car, she has an apartment, she's been a ski bum. Her father has a minka with a split bamboo ceiling and memories of Shinto priests and fire gods. Her nonchalance suggests intimacy: smoking cigarettes, going out for coffee, returning for a languorous romp on the floor. Adam sleeps in boxers in case his mother barges in to collect his laundry; he works at Subway and has never been on a plane. He squirms, unable to respond, until he yawns loudly and announces, "Time for a brewski."

Does she know she's showing off?

*

On the Internet, you can find anyone: old flames, lonely cons, even Scandinavians with shared afflictions. I have located Franz, who is philosophical about our condition.

> Welcome to the club, Franz messages.

> I discovered I was totally mirrored inside when I enlisted in the Swiss army. The doctors told me. There was no indication before. I believe I am better than the ordinary man at most everything :) it's a funny trick that nature has pulled :) that's all.

Thanks for your input, Franz. I am typing. This is all new to me.

> It takes time to understand but you will be fine. I am a ski racer :) Last week I raced a 20 K at Engardin. I consider it a genetic improvement :)

Do you think I will have health problems? My doctor has told me nothing.

> It's unlikely that you have any complications since they usually surface as a child. About 3 to 5% of the people with *situs inversus* have heart problems (compared to 1% of the general population.) About 25% of the people with SI have a condition known as Kartagener's syndrome, which leads to increased respiratory infections. I am hardly ever sick :) Around here, I am known as the healthy one :) Were you healthy?

Yes, I type, relieved.

> Then you are fine. There is not much information out there :) I would someday like to know more. It seems like a strange trick to pull. Yes?

Franz will send me a photo, he says, and asks for one of me. Last week, I stood in my lecture hall—an open scallop shell with rows of seats—and paced the width at twenty-two steps, which was supposed to tell me something.

*

After his retirement, my father became a gentleman host on cruise ships. The agency called them "knights of the sea," which reminded me of a brand of tuna. He was charged with dining and dancing with single women, who outnumbered the men eight to one.

Each time he left, he packed a dinner jacket, dancing shoes and tan trousers which my mother pressed. Forever penitent, she shrugged, "It gives him something to do," as though he was filling grocery bags or carving decoys. "Walter likes to work."

Really?

"He could *never* sit still. He has too much energy."

The job fuelled my father's ego and allowed him to see the South Pacific, the Caribbean and once, although he hated it, Alaska. The job cost him two hundred dollars US a week, and required him to dance seven hours a day. The rest was free. To be accepted, he had to prove he was proficient in the rumba, foxtrot, swing waltz and cha-cha, and that he was a widower, a lie my mother accepted even though it buried her alive.

"What difference does it make?" she would ask.

My father thrived in the kitschy cruise ship atmosphere where people imagined they were debonair and worldly. Occasionally, he would get postcards from dolls he had met on cruises. My mother would place them on the kitchen table with the power bill. It was against the rules, my father insisted, lest anyone question the integrity of his job, to "do things" with the guests. "It's all on the up and up." My mother nodded her assent. I remember a card from Delores, who started her note with "Hello Cutey."

✶

I am in my office reading course appraisals, written anonymously then transcribed for profs. When I was young, you stood behind your beliefs, none of this anonymity. Through the wall to Sneddon's office, I feel a disconcerting emptiness, a void that threatens to suck me in, like a plane door kicked open. At the expense of everything else, Sneddon spends hours in audio stores, testing speakers, subwoofers and amps, buying obscure recordings of frightful singers. What, I wonder, is he hoping to hear? The voice of God, the Quran revealed through Muhammad?

Last night, I flew to the head of the Tasman Glacier in New Zealand, where I surveyed the landscape of ice caves and glacial canyons. Everything was so fantastic that it looked computer-generated. I breathed the sharp air. Just as I strapped on my avalanche beeper, I spotted the homicidal students from the hallway, the ones who had snubbed me. I offered a cavalier wave before I pushed off, schussing down the course.

I pull out the student responses. Does Sneddon even look at his, frantic now that his CDs are disintegrating with pinpricks?

Through grammatical clues, pet phrases and social references, I can match each appraisal with its student author. Incomplete sentences: Darla, the vegan straight-edge with the annoying x on her hand. Another reference to Al Capone: Chad in the trucker's hat. I scan, not reading, just looking looking until I see "brilliant," Sarah's adjective of choice. I pause, as though I have stumbled upon a diary, wondering whether to read on or avert my eyes.

"Nothing brilliant or illuminating. Not as interesting as first term when we explored the bittersweet life of Anna Swan with Professor Sneddon."

The words hit my gut, and suddenly I am in grade school and a nun is strapping me for wearing boots to class, and I choke back tears of humiliation, knowing I don't own shoes. I hear a knock and see Adam, round-faced, carrying a Beastie Boys backpack. I give myself a moment to calm my hand.

✳

BEATRICE'S NOTEBOOK:

Years ago, when I had trouble falling asleep, I counted men the way insomniacs count sheep. Only men I had kissed, most in one blurry year, placing them in chronological order.

First there was Greg, a phys. ed student. Then Gerry, then Dennis.

I kissed them all without expectations or regrets.

I met Andrew in the campus bookstore, Sociology section, under Engels. He acted intrigued by my umbrella, Starry Nights *with a wooden handle. Andrew walked me to my dorm and we kissed on the step for twenty minutes. He asked for my number, but never called. I didn't care.*

By then, I had kissed Nicky. I spotted him weaving through a dance playing a flute like Ian Anderson of Jethro Tull. In red, he was incandescent with straight hair and the fine neck of a deer. I had bought a new outfit for the dance: dusty pink cords that flared over platform shoes and a clingy bodysuit that snapped under the crotch. Emboldened by vodka and orange, I strolled by Nicky three times until he tapped my shoulder and asked me to dance.

Nicky and I left the spell of Procol Harum in his car, a beater with a red canoe strapped on top. Nicky said he was a med student, a wasted lie, since the truth was more appealing to me: he was in art school. Off we drove, to a party, then a beach, where we kissed.

Two months later, I kissed Andrew again. Dick came next. A dreadful kisser, my only mistake.

"What could you expect," asked my friend, "from a guy named Dick?"

And now my friend has called from Louisiana where she lives with her husband, an art professor. "Do you remember Nicky from university, the guy with the flute? I met a painter at a party and his name came up.... He's dying."

In cyberspace, I search for the incandescent Nicky. Let me see him, I whisper, let me find the life I hope he had. I capture him on a web page, older but vaguely the same, his face the tan of tea stains. He is celebrated, I discover. He has won awards painting landscapes in a high-realism style, lush, glazed scenes surprisingly *still. It is the stillness that bewilders me. I expected colour-charged abstracts moving in all directions like Nicky and his flute, or Chagall fantasies fuelled by fairies.*

My husband is in the doorway, vexed. I know he has something to tell me, something that has been troubling him. Humbled by the delicacy of life, I smile at his optimism, at the soft lens he saves for people like Bernie and, possibly, me.

"I'm going to try to save Adam."

"That's great," I nod. "I knew you would." Beatrice.

*

I remember the day my mother took me to Pine Grove Park. The air was damp and scented with pine. Stone still, I stood in a clearing, hand outstretched and laden with seeds, waiting for chickadees. When one landed, it was so delightful that my knees buckled and my hand shook.

My mother took a photo, later framed, of a boy, a bird and a Mary Maxim sweater with jets on the back. When the chickadee landed, I was surprised by how firmly it wrapped its tiny feet around my finger. Mother said it wouldn't eat my seeds, it would stash them in bark, dead leaves and knotholes, and return in winter when food was scarce. I was happy that Mother was pleased.

All my life, I have felt as though I am in a rushing stream, fighting to keep from slipping on the greasy rocks beneath me, into the familial descent that seems as predestined as death. Now, I am steady.

Franz has emailed me a photo from a ski hill. He has wild eyes, and his arm is around a hammy man in a horned helmet and face paint. In the background, I see mauve mountains and a train that could be going anywhere. I send him one of me, nebbish in glasses. I look like the man in the aqua-fitness class, I realize with a jolt, the one with the secrets.

The Watermelon Social

My house makes me cry.

It is an executive split built during that collective lapse in taste known as the seventies. When we moved in, one wall was covered with barnboards, swag lamps cast a queasy light. Everything was brown and cavernous, like a subterranean restaurant that specializes in Wiener schnitzel and German plonk.

"It's splendid," declared my husband, who bought the house while I was postpartum, a free-running creature drifting in and out of phase with the natural world. "Look at all the space."

The original owners, the Sandersons, fled after a wife-swapping debacle that left grease on the walls and cigarette burns in the bedroom. A casualty of divorce, neglected during the final days, my house reeked of damaged children and Singapore slings. Outraged, as though I had foregone the seventies, as though I had never worn hot pants or owned a Vega wagon, I cursed the Sandersons for their bad taste and cheap morals, which had contributed equally, I insisted, to their divorce and my home's fondue stains.

I go to the kitchen. There is no symmetry to a split, just a surrealistic discord of stairs. My house has no windows on the side, just the front and back where the sun never hits. "Why do you want side windows?" asked my husband. Last winter, as days shortened and SAD set in, I painted two rooms hysterical yellow, thinking sunlight, but somehow the brown, like mildew or sadness, couldn't be covered.

My son appears in the doorway, collecting himself after preschool.

"John's mother brought his new baby to school this morning."

"Hmmmm. How was he?"

"I think he was fake."

"Really?"

"Hmmm." He nods seriously. "He didn't move, he just laid there."

"Maybe he was sleeping?"

"No, Mom, he was fake."

"Okay," I shrug.

We look out a window at a grid of splits. When I moved in, I thought there was no one home, that everyone worked, but then I discovered the houses were full of women. Like the Borrowers, their motto was to never be seen. They stayed in until dusk, or slipped through remote-control garages, hiding from the street, a street owned by quiet, an oppressive dead that skews your senses and blows your circadian rhythm.

In two years, I have never heard a child cry or an adult laugh. I have never seen a tossed football or a game of tag. My children move in a world of whispers and nudges. I've never known a place with so much power, a place this ordinary and unassuming. *Be quiet*, it orders. *You are making too much noise*. I try to explain this to my husband, but he can't understand.

"Let the kids make as much noise as they want. We pay taxes!"

"You don't feel it. It's like telling a joke at a funeral."

He looks at me as if I am mad, one of those kooks who stared at a Tim Hortons wall in Cape Breton until they saw the Virgin Mary. I thought suburbia would be streets of laughing kids, racing bikes and backyards without fences, mothers trading recipes, carpooling to soccer, commiserating over measles.

"Hurry up, Mom," my daughter urges. "The watermelon will be gone."

"What's the point of a watermelon social—" I find it excruciating to say those last two words; they stick in my mouth, like *domestic engineer*, or *puppy love*, "if there's no watermelon?"

"C'mon, Mom. Hurry up!"

We enter Greendale Elementary, a stucco institution of high standards and three hundred students, a launch pad for science fairs and piano recitals. The air is smug and claustrophobic.

I hand a toonie to a woman in a denim dress, an impenetrable blue habit. Her name is Marilyn. She is a volunteer, the über mom, proud parent of Gregory and Devon, star Greendale grads, and the baby, Virginia. Brought out of retirement, propped up, properly medicated, she seems determined to last the evening. For the volunteers, the watermelon social is a no-brainer. Even the old war horses easing out to pasture with the fourth child, exhausted by fifteen years of do-erism, drained by field trips and croup, leave their dark houses for the social. Two social hours are worth thirty-eight weeks of toil in the computer lab, four months of library, eight batches of Harry Potter cupcakes. The social volunteers are thanked by name in the school newsletter, posted in the lobby. Everyone sees you in your alphabet sweater and your most beatific smile. It doesn't matter if it's your only appearance all year, if you have sunk into a menopausal abyss of gin and regrets, if you never wash your hair or sleep with your husband, if you make crank calls to your teenage son's girlfriend who is taking up all his time. It doesn't matter: it is the social.

Down the hall, a buff woman admires a leaf collage. "Ahh," she exclaims theatrically. Her pale bespectacled daughter sucks her fingers.

"Who's that woman with Meagen?" my daughter asks.

"That's her mother."

I have seen the mother running in a spandex bra and shorts, a water bottle strapped to her back. A "Just Do It" ad, defying the code of stillness. A sallow man admires the mother, new to the neighbourhood, a non-volunteer.

"Well, who's the woman I always see her with?" my daughter insists.

"That's the *babysitter*." I drag the word out like a threat.

The sallow man, I realize, is Marilyn's husband, an expert on plankton. His name is Gerald. In recent years, he has become invisible, a mute walker who ignores her histrionics and lives in a secret world of sci-fi novels and CNN. Gerald is a skinny man who has lost all pigment in his body. His hair is preternaturally white, his skin the colour of unbleached paper. He could be sold in an environmental store, underfed, uncoloured, placing no burden on the ecosystem. He rides a bicycle and probably doesn't sweat. She, on the other hand, is a tornado of angst, nearing the end of her run. Marilyn has spent twenty years courting teachers, typing projects, collecting Canadian Tire money for tambourines, always checking her progress against others.

✶

We enter the gym, a pastiche of preening parents and darting kids. Greendale Elementary Is a Place for Friends to Help, the motto disingenuously announces. The dozen teachers are spread about like eggs in a scavenger hunt.

"Ahhhhh. This is refreshing!" A sweater-vested man grins as watermelon juice drips into his beard. He spits seeds into a paper napkin, keeping one eye on a teacher, ready to pounce.

"It used to be an ice cream social," a stout volunteer named Sally explains, "but we switched to watermelon."

"Uh huh?"

"Lactose intolerance."

Sally is wearing a sleeveless top and a white skirt that exposes her legs, purple stumps covered with a lichen of broken veins and stretch marks. Her stomach bulges against the distended skirt, sweat drips from her armpits like battery acid. When she smiles maniacally, her face cracks like a ventriloquist's dummy and my son grabs my hand.

"That's prudent," the man nods, and just then, just as he takes his eye off the teacher, Sally shoots in to fill the void. "I'm Dylan's mom," she exhales. "Surprise!"

Outmanoeuvred, distracted by the small talk, the man swallows a seed. For a bulb-shaped woman with the flush of high blood pressure, Sally is uncommonly swift. "Dylan looooooooooves Grade Three. He and Warren live for dioramas."

On Sally's shoulders rests a huge pumpkin. Her eyes are

slits carved into the fleshy pulp, her mouth is a gigantic slash, a canyon of teeth and gums that opens so wide you can see the desperation. Sally's husband, Warren, is a gym teacher who earns as much as a postal worker and sweats through each round of layoffs. He and the girls are monochromatic, brown and dull as dried leaves. I wonder if they ever had life, laughter or chlorophyll running through their veins. Sally is a school fixture, the mini-Marilyn, making paper, Ukrainian eggs, origami frogs and all of the scenery for the Grade Six production of *Sleeping Beauty*. Last year, Dylan, "a special learner," killed the Grade Two hamster.

"Dioramas are lovely," says Mrs. Green, the teacher.

Sally laughs maniacally. Ha ha ha. Mouth open, she throws back the huge head. Ha ha ha. The laughter pushes up against the teacher like a barroom drunk, a sodden hooligan, and Mrs. Green nervously laughs with her.

*

I am not listening; I am looking at Sally's pumpkin head. Something odd is happening to women my age, a genetic fluke like the preponderance of six-foot girls and the birth of quads, an insidious trend that goes unobserved until you look up and notice that every single girl in the Gap towers over you.

Women my age are sprouting beards. Sally's starts at one ear and trails to her double chin, where it culminates in three witch's hairs. Despite her girth, she can't be over forty, I think, and the beard is blonde. Aren't beards and moustaches the domain of swarthy Italians and stout Lebanese, dark women who celebrate Our Lady of Fatima and dutifully clean the church for Father O'Flynn? Or Nana's cleaning lady, Maria, who wore red sneakers, complained of chest pains and stashed away enough unreported income to buy a retirement villa in Portugal? Did blonde women in their forties really grow beards?

"Oh no," someone screams. "Oh no!"

"The watermelon."

"Daniel!"

A shriek splits the air like a thunderclap, and a boy runs through the gym, waving his arms. Ducking parents, a woman in a corduroy jumper gives chase, face frozen into a blank mask of paralyzed emotions, too potent to release.

"That's Daniel," says my daughter.

"Oh." I follow the woman with my eyes.

Behind us, the principal is righting the toppled table. "It's no problem," he says too loudly. Watermelon seeds glisten like shiny black bugs and juice dribbles onto the hardwood floor that pleads "No Black-soled Shoes." Split open, the red fleshy fruit looks obscene.

Where is Mr. Tarnapolski, the school custodian who ran a marathon last spring, and who is often called upon to chase down Daniel when his inner voices say "Bolt" and he dashes from the classroom, through the fingers of his designated helper and out the door? Can somebody find Mr. Tarnapolski? Can somebody please find him? I see Sally shake her head back and forth, back and forth.

"Do you work outside the home?" Gerald asks me.

I'm telling you all this because it's important.

✶

My husband is a TV field producer, which means he is never home for watermelon socials. He follows the news to strange and mundane locations, where he meets pros and wannabes like Jimmy Belliveau Freelance Fire Photographer, whose card reads, "Find 'em Hot and Leave 'em Dripping."

Today my husband is home and cranky. The office phoned at two a.m., scaring my son. One of the conceits of the producer is that he is always ready, poised to drop everything for the next big story. To facilitate this, he must be kept aware of news, where and when it is breaking. Editors who have been chewed out for failing to stir the sleeping producer, desk-bound drones counting the days until retirement, have a way of getting even. They phone for nothing.

"Ah, sorry Dan, but I see a note saying the premier is having a newser tomorrow on recycling. Gee, you weren't asleep, were you?"

"Ahhhhh, no."

"Ohhh, geez. It is two o'clock, isn't it? I've been so busy I didn't notice."

As my husband makes a coffee, he scans the paper. I try to tell him about Gerald and the watermelon social but he sighs and wonders why I "would even care about those people." Oh, he mentions absently at the sports section, I ran into Gerry Webb at the rare wine store, where Gerry was buying a great Australian that he tried last month in blah blah blah. He asked how you were and I told him you were writing a book.

I look up, stunned. "Writing a book?"

"I didn't want him thinking you were just at home."

"Well, I am. When would I…?"

"I just … " he sighs. "*Those* people don't understand."

"What happens if he asks me about my book?"

He sighs again. "You're right. I'm sorry."

"The book that never gets published."

"He won't ask."
"Of course he will."
"How many first novels are published anyway?"

⁎

I look in the mirror, practising my encounter with Gerry, a binge drinker who once fired a starter's pistol in the newsroom where we worked. A forty-five-year-old woman in sweats attempts a knowing smirk. "A book? Yeah, it's a tell-all, Gerry. You better be worried." Gerry mutters something about rehab. I smirk again and wonder why I look so stupid.

In my mind's eye, I am tall, lean, bare to life's emotions. Being raw-boned implies an elegance that can carry jeans and sneakers. Raw-boned doesn't need the camouflage of high heels, big hair or shoulder pads; it screams bohemian indifference. I have always loved stripped-down men, angular, long-haired. In grad school, I met a six-foot-three swimmer with an impossible waist, who held me close over the flame of our overwrought poems, squeezed my torso and whispered, "Oh, oh" at the inch of offending flesh. The inch has always been there and always will be. I have never looked as though I was suffering for art or love. Always, I longed to be spare and free, unencumbered, a twig drifting downstream, a modernist beach house with bare windows and wooden beams. To sit on the floor and cross my legs, yoga style, or wear my hair straight and flat. Maybe in a chignon.

I married a sapling with straight hair and a delicate neck. We met at an all-night Fassbinder fest, where he raved about the director's use of mirrors, curtains and shadows. For a while, he smoked Russian cigarettes and argued that *Veronika Voss* was more succinctly ironic than

The Marriage of Maria Braun. I thought he would never grow fat, just lean and tired from the burden of his emotions. To my surprise, he developed a beer belly but stayed as melodramatic as his cinematic hero. My husband's neck stiffens as he opens the fridge; he grimaces: Miracle Whip instead of mayo. Didn't I know the mustard had to be Dijon, the sliced ham black and smoked?

"The kids like Miracle Whip," I explain, trying to shed light on my world.

"That's because that's all they've tried."

"No, they like Miracle Whip."

"Whatever," he sighs.

Outside, the sun is shining. The mound of snow by the driveway has vanished, exposing twelve timid crocuses. Small rocks and gravel have appeared from nowhere, like coins in the back of a couch. They cover the bleached grass, the driveway; they stick to my shoes and hitch rides inside.

My son sits at the kitchen table, excited. It is career week at preschool and one of the fathers visited this morning. He was a helicopter pilot, my son explains, and he brought in a ceremonial sword, which the children touched.

"I think it was real gold," he says.

"He wasn't a pilot, he was a navigator," my daughter interrupts. How would she know? She wasn't even there.

"It *was* real gold," my son decides. He picks up a slice of apple.

"Did anyone ask any questions?" I inquire, and think about the sunshine. Fat-breasted robins have filled the trees; the spiky heads of the crocuses remind me of punk haircuts. My kitchen is now the colour of a Granny Smith apple, a tart shade that covers the Sandersons' sins.

"One boy asked, 'Who is your best friend at work'?"

"Really?"

"He asked everyone the same question all week."

"Do you think he'll ask Daddy when he comes in?"

He shrugs his shoulders, and he smells like love. I touch his soft blond head and I ache with the fragility of life. Unlike my daughter, he is shy, a watcher. My heart breaks with his doubts and I want to make them vanish, I want to make him strong. I know I fear too much, but they are a mother's fears, a mother's love, a mother's curse that even little boys as precious as he is come without guarantees.

"It was him, Mom," my daughter says loudly, pointing at my son. "Sarah Mosher told me. *He* asked them all."

The store feels like an underground bunker, a survivalist camp of cheap CDs and polypropylene pants. The metal racks around us groan, overloaded with no-name jeans from China and women's tops that soar to an oversize twenty-four.

"I know it's here somewhere," I mutter, peering around a stack of plastic sandals. "I saw it in the flyer."

"Can we go see the goldfish?" my son asks.

"Hmmm?"

"The goldfish in the tanks."

"They killed them all," my daughter whispers. "Remember?"

When I look at my son, his hair is olive. The fluorescent lights are so powerful they make you squint; magically, they turn everything green. Lime-coloured and overexposed, we march on, looking for muffin tins, past the

$19.99 comforters that scratch like horsehair and the blankets that come in an incongruous square: four feet by four.

We stop at an opening in the racks. The air smells like new tires, a ripe odour that overpowers the gift soaps and seeps into Ladies' Wear. My son is thinking about the fish, I can tell; my daughter is explaining filters.

Before us, in a wasteland of scorched plastic, lies an oasis of six tables and lukewarm tea. Under the merciless lights, I can see a buffet of sealed sandwiches and Jello dotted with Reddi-wip. The food looks like the rubber hamburgers I used to buy my dog, petrified food to masticate and maul. The cafeteria has no business being here, I think, in a place this overexposed, a place that smells like tires. Eight girls are gathered at two tables for what appears to be a birthday party, a stagnant, lonely scene that reminds me of an Edward Hopper painting.

A worn woman is passing gifts to the birthday girl, who is wearing a Britney Spears belly top. A disconnected guest picks stuffing from her chair.

"Let's go," I order, running from the sight. Before we can be gobbled up by hopelessness, we rush to checkout, clutching peanuts. Our line is stalled. A woman has lost her Frequent Shopper card and wants to give the bonus points to her friend. "They are not transferable," the clerk declares sternly, as though she is ruling on something important, like bone marrow or a liver.

I look to the next lane, pretending not to hear, and see a clerk scanning a licence plate. "That's wrong," her customer insists. "I know it's on for two ninety nine." The clerk drops the "Sexy Mama" plate and lifts a microphone for a price check. Her voice cracks, unaccustomed to the mike. "Lane Six, I need a price check on novelties," she says, and I stare at her loose jaw and grey hair, trying to bring her into focus. I close one eye, the other; I read the tag on the Cheap 'N Easy smock. It is Marilyn, doyenne of the Home and School, proud mother of Gregory, Devon and Virginia. What is she doing here, in this paranoid bunker of canned beans and bingo markers? She has at least one degree in pharmacy and she worked in the Main Street Professional Building before she met Gerald at a computer workshop, got married and raised three perfect kids. "Would you be interested," she asks the sexy mama, "in the family portrait special?"

My daughter comes home from school with a papier mâché puppet and a notice on ringworm. That volunteer, the one named Sally, was in her class this morning. In a loud voice, she had asked Virginia, "Does your mother have a job?"

"Don't tell anyone, Mom," my daughter whispers. "Virginia said her brother lost all the family's money in the stock market."

"What?" I scoff. Gregory is Marilyn's validation, a pre-med student, a Big Brother who made the dean's list. "How could he get all their money?"

"I don't know. That's what Virginia said."

The news spreads through the neighbourhood, through the petrified streets and motionless houses; it bounces off fireplaces and creeps into bedrooms. I can hear the sharp intake of breath. I can see Sally charging into school, nostrils flared, mouth twisted to a sneer. All the bones in her face have dissolved, as if dipped in a vat of venom, and all that remain are fat and jowls and blind retribution. Last month, just before Valentine's Day, just before Marilyn's long-service award at the Home and School, just before

Devon's violin solo at the Metro Music Festival, just before Dr. Zimmer changed her estrogen prescription, Gerald turned to her and said, "After twenty-two years, your free lunch is over."

✳

I am sitting in a plastic chair, poolside. My husband is in Florida covering a hurricane and we have checked into a motel near home to test the waterslide. I try not to imagine Marilyn scanning novelty plates, tables turned by the treacherous Gerald, uncoloured, underfed, but no longer mute. I try not to think about life or choices or risks.

Near the entrance, next to the towels, is a water cooler with paper cups. Over and over, a human yo-yo, my son drains a cone-shaped cup, drops it in the garbage and springs back for more. "I'm thirsty," he says when I tell him he may pee his pants. My daughter is swimming, synchro-style, one hand over her head, up and down the ten-metre pool, keeping her cup dry.

I think about how the peace can be punctured. Last week, the kids were playing library, my son methodically checking out my daughter's selections. He had a stamp pad and a card for each borrowed book.

"I'd like something on cats," my daughter announced.

"Cats?" he mused, scanning his shelves. "Ummmmm. We have *Puss 'n Boots* and *Garfield's Christmas*." I could feel his sense of quiet accomplishment as he stamped the cards. All went smoothly, until there was a flap over something and my daughter slammed down a copy of *The Secret Garden*.

"You are a terrible librarian," she barked. "You don't even help your customers." I wanted to laugh at the foolishness of the charge, but when I looked across the room, my son was crying, big hard tears that he tried to hide by burying his face in his chest, heartbroken tears that cut to his soul.

Now, he is smiling. So I leave him to his water. I leave him, calm and protected, to his task.

The Year of the Horse

Lowe, Georgie, 46, died of natural causes.

Born in Moose Village, N.S., he was the son of Edgar and Rose (Lowe).

He enjoyed the outdoors and listening to music on his car radio. His remains have been cremated.

-30 -

"Is that it?" begs Melody. "Fini?"

"That's all she wrote," says the funeral home.

"All right," she sighs into the newsroom phone. "Grrrrrracias."

Through a haze of smoke and twang, Melody sees a picnic table bolted to the back of a pickup. She sees Georgie peering through the iced windshield of an '82 Honda that sweats when it rains. Newspaper floor mats, duct-taped seats. Melody stares until the letters shift, an anagram of death, until it's all as clear as a Travis Tritt song: Georgie Lowe, Gigolo!

"I had a cat named Georgie," Melody informs her computer. "He wasn't a gigolo, but he had exceptional powers. He could tell the future with a Ouija board. My Uncle Roy was a gigolo although my mother denied it even after Father died. She claimed he was a dance instructor. Before *my* Georgie was abducted, he said I would travel far, meet a dark stranger named Jesus and learn to ride a horse."

Click. Melody teleports Georgie to Merle, the myopic editor, who toils like a bricklayer stacking the dearly departed around ads. Georgie is wearing a blousy jacket cinched at the waist, a red-white-and-blue homage to the National Hot Rod Association. Merle is a collage of grey.

"Let's see." Melody opens her file, started at seven p.m. with a call from Darling's Funeral Home. "Hmmmm." Melody scrolls down, an exquisite duck with an upturned nose. Merle is into the alphabet, she knows, which will place Georgie Lowe between Dr. F. A. Leifert, MD OC, 82, of Halifax and Catherine May, 71, of Bedford.

Oh my. What would they have in common?

Mrs. May was born in the Year of the Sheep, making her elegant and accomplished in the arts. She would understand *sfumato* and the Dada movement. Soaring on a magic carpet of privilege, Dr. Leifert would have a lofty view of the underclass. Georgie would appear flushed in a trucker's cap, missing incisors and one critical chromosome. Georgie didn't mind not having money; he simply couldn't bear the sadness of being poor, the way it wore you down like shingles. Georgie envied the crooks and con men. He liked the way they strutted into the AAA Pawn Shop and came out grinning. Georgie imagined the con man's house at Christmas: there would be gifts, beer and jokes. The con man would hand out presents, smile, and never once snap from sadness, never once beat the crap out of a five-year-old boy who had stepped on an Etch a Sketch. "Do you know what that cost, you no good little bastard?" A con man would never snap and stumble off in tears.

Her Georgie was orange, and knowing as a Buddha, and when he stared at you, his eyes were shrewd, somnolent slits. Father said Georgie was wise; he knew that life was a staggered start with misplaced intervals. For some, the race was over before it began.

"Hi, Melody." It's Jim, the hockey reporter. "Many stiffs?"

"*Comme ci comme ça*," clucks Melody in red hipster pants.

Like a Lichtenstein canvas, Melody is all primary colours. Her hair is yellow, the same shade as fishermen's oils. Under the yellow hair are cobalt eyes that flash, iridescent eyes with rechargeable batteries. Jim's sister had a troll doll with eyes like that. You squeezed its belly and the eyes lit up. These are the eyes of a woman who would paint stars on her ceiling, smile at leaping unicorns and cats with mittens. "Ahh, so much to ponder, with Prometheus and Odysseus to blame." Melody speaks a foreign language, animated images linked by whimsy. Amused, Jim wants to respond, to validate her spirit, but can't. Nothing, he realizes, makes sense.

"If anyone calls," says Jim with an invisible wink, "the game went into triple overtime."

Jim is wearing his leather Roots jacket, which means he's headed for the bar and a night of debauchery. He smells of aftershave and disappointed women. Jim should mellow, thinks Melody, or end up like Uncle Roy, compelled to live with Grandma.

"Time is adventitious.…"

"Hey." Jim leans close and smiles. "Chillax."

Chillax is the mantra of the night shift, a society of insomniacs, burnouts and rookies. At night, the newsroom goes shoeless, plays solitaire and orders pizza, shielded from scrutiny by locked doors and a moat of darkness. Ja Rule raps through Sports, and Elizabeth Mooney's teacup poodle, Nana, yaps out loud. Last week, the petulant

Nana peed on Jim's hockey bag, proof, said Elizabeth, that Jim was incorrigible. Reporters dash in and out from assignments, heads down like lapsed churchgoers at Christmas Mass.

✳

"Obits. Melody speaking."
"Hello, this is Pye's Funeral Home."
"Ahh, you've had a busy day."
"Yep, a patch of black ice near the legion. But this one is from away."

> Levy, Carl, 31, died in Calgary.
> Born in Halibut Point, he was the son of Billy and Mabel (Cahoon).
> He enjoyed visiting Canadian Tire and taking care of his dogs. Carl had a good way with people and dogs. Carl was a friend of Bill W.
> He is survived by his stepbrother Sherman.

"Did you know that Rhodesian Ridgebacks used to hunt tigers?" asks Melody.
"That's an interesting fact," says Mr. Pye.
Melody knows she talks too much, but that is natural for the Year of the Horse. Carl Levy. Another L, in with Dr. Leifert and his suffocating degrees. Dr. Leifert had a signet ring, a lineage and the astringent face of a German tennis pro. Melody's pulse races. How could he not diminish the canine-loving Carl?

✳

The elevator opens for a dark-skinned man in a midnight shirt. He's holding a paper in his hand as if it's meaningful: military orders or a manifesto. Catching his breath, he gazes at Melody, a lanky gamine in a pixie cut.

"Hello," he says.

"*Buenos dias.*" She smells like wildflowers.

The man smiles as though he's met an old friend in a bar, where time melts and reggae music erases the ravages of war. Melody hears laughter, she sees a volcano belch and steam, demanding sacrifices for the goddess of fire. Melody rises to greet him. Under one sleeve is a leather bracelet that complements his accent. He looks Latin to Melody, dark and sultry as Jimmy Smits. His movements are mannered, European, as if he is on the verge of dabbing the corners of his lips with a linen napkin. He has the fine hands of a jeweller.

"I have something for you."

"*Gracias.*"

They talk, and Melody asks, although she knows the answer, "Where are you from?"

"Nicaarrrrrragua."

"Why are you here?"

He laughs and closes his eyes as if he is hearing music. Ahh, the Nicaraguans, thinks Melody. In four hundred years, the Spanish and Indian blood have mixed to make such beautiful people, mestizo.

"I am a poet."

"Ahhhhhh," nods Melody, who knows the truth is like a mudslide, moving, morphing as it surges by. What you see depends on where you stand, how close you are to being sucked in, smothered. You can't catch the truth, hold it to your chest.

The man rattles his *rrr*s as though he is clearing his throat of a furball. Melody thinks of maracas, then Bianca Jagger in her white wedding hat, more exquisite than Mick. She imagines swimming in spring-fed lagunas and dancing at fiestas patronales. Melody decides his name is Jesus—Hay Zoo—pronounced like a Latin ballplayer. She doesn't know if it's Nicaraguan, but she likes the sound, Hay Zoo, Hey You, a children's rhyme. Melody is floating, dandelion seeds blown into the wind.

*

    Levy, Carl (Buckaroo), 31, rode his pony out of this world and into the next.
    Born in Halibut Point, Buckaroo left Nova Scotia in the seventies for the Alberta oil fields. Out west, Carl visited a ranch where he discovered an unnatural aptitude with animals.
    Soon, Buckaroo was a regular on the rodeo circuit, renowned for his flowing blond hair and daredevil moves. The Bluenose Bomber was one of his nicknames. In an age of specialists, he could do it all. He was a national runner-up in saddle bronc riding and he was a perennial threat in bull riding. It was believed that Carl had mastered the language of horses, communicating with a vocabulary of grunts, nods and whinnies.
    The rodeo community was in mourning this week after Buckaroo died in Calgary, crushed by a bull.
    For a while, Carl was linked with Madonna, who told reporters, "I'd love to get Buckaroo in the saddle." Carl shed the caustic pop star and married Mary Anne Smith of Montana, a beautiful trick rider. With their earnings, they bought a Texas ranch that became a breeding farm and a retreat for abused children.
    Carl's career stalled for six months when he underwent reconstructive surgery on his knee. Buckaroo sustained those injuries when he was attacked by Beelzebub, the meanest, most feared bull on the circuit. Some believed Beelzebub was possessed. Tragically, it was Beelzebub who also delivered the fatal wound.
    Buckaroo's remains were cremated and scattered over his farm. "Happy Trails, Old Cowboy. I'll see you at the next sunset." Condolences can be sent online to mourners@atlantic.ca.
- 30-

Click. Melody releases the obit to Merle. Over the years, Merle's senses have shut down, leaving him flat and still as a well. Deprived of light and air, he rations his energy and moves like a man no longer waiting to be rescued.

Trudeau was prime minister when Merle started nights; Elvis was alive.

Merle was put on the overnight shift to babysit Art Connolly, an alcoholic editor and celebrated trivia buff. Art's family had some influence, as mysterious as the Masons, which the newsroom never fathomed. Without a sitter, Art would make obscene phone calls and escape to fern bars. Art died ten years ago, but by then, the paper had forgotten about Merle, buried alive on overnights, like the Toltec Indians of Central America, left to ponder life's deepest questions.

Melody hears a beep, an email at mourners@atlantic.ca.

> Accept my condolences on the death of Buckaroo Levy. While his life may have been short, it was full and vibrant, an inspiration to us all.

Another beep. Her cobalt eyes flash with vindication.

> I saw Buckaroo at a rodeo in Montana; it made me proud to be a Bluenoser. Goddamn you, Beelzebub.

Merle is talking to his son, Graham, visiting in a MIS-FITS T-shirt. Somewhere along the way, while Merle was sleeping or chasing Art Connolly into the can, Graham became a busker, a move he explains to Jim, the hockey reporter, with a sincerity that makes Merle ache.

"Now, what's that involve?" asks Jim, feigning interest.

"Mainly juggling, which is the foundation for all busking, although The Great Grape Jello forgot that, denouncing his roots, and ... excuse me, I'm drifting into buskerese."

"Buskerese, eh?" Jim is tall and stupidly handsome.

"Occupational hazard. Like fire. I had a little accident recently, lost my eyebrows."

Jim inches away. "Whatever gets you through the night."

"Exactly!"

"For me it happens to be cheap blondes and tequila, but if fire is your thing...."

"It is for now."

"Well, good luck, buddy." Jim slaps Graham's back.

"Why thanks!" Graham takes the brush-off literally. "I'm not finding a cure for AIDS, but what I do makes a difference to a lot of people."

Slowly, as if it hurts to move, Merle makes his way to Melody.

"I got a call from an old buzzard," he says. "She's from Halibut Point, and she was asking about this Carl Levy."

"Oh?"

"I called the funeral homes, Darling's, Waters."

"It was brought in by hand."

"Okay." Merle shrugs.

"We've received several emails."

Merle is no longer listening. He has followed a sigh to purgatory where Elizabeth edits the wedding page in sweatpants. Merle remembers when Elizabeth wore belted dresses, when she strode into News with a British education and the collected works of Oscar Wilde. Back then, the wedding page was reserved for studio poses of brides and grooms, fiftieth-anniversary shots of regal seniors. Under an advertising edict, the gates have been opened. Last week, Lance and Greg announced their engagement in a hot tub. Smokes, raccoons, illegitimate children and neck tattoos have stormed the page like Russian peasants, coarse-faced Bolsheviks, drunk and desecrating churches. Today, Linda and Dauwayne are standing by a Viking deep-freeze full of rabbits. Dauwayne is icy, Linda achingly acquiescent.

> On our 12th anniversary, I know our souls are forever linked like Siamese twins. I still love you. Linda.

Dauwayne has bolted, but Linda, with $69.95 and a cherished photo, is pleading with the callous fugitive. Ambush ads, Elizabeth calls the atrocities, which she treats like party crashers, boors who pee in planters and leave with the family Hummels. In protest, Elizabeth has chopped her hair into an orange pageboy that sits atop her ample face like a yarmulke. Irregular, the bangs look like Barbie bangs hacked off by an impulsive owner. Sprite-like, elfin, the yarmulke is a joke she flaunts with contempt.

"When I was a kid," Merle says deliberately, turning his back on Elizabeth, "my uncle went to the Calgary Stampede and brought back a book full of pictures of cowboys and bulls and chuckwagon races. To me, it was like the Sears Christmas catalogue. Did you know that with stampede stock, the foals are named alphabetically by the year they are born? In '91, all the names start with B, in '92 with C, and so on."

Merle pauses, imagining a row of alphabetical foals. "Whenever possible, I like to read about horses."

✳

It's four p.m. at the Shore's Delight Motel, and the pool

is as flat as a striker bed. A family hobbles onto the deck under a canopy of chlorine and mist.

Melody, home to see her mother, knows the Burgoynes. They have a double-wide down the road, on a lot alive with whirling birds and planters made from Javex bottles. From her mother's house, Melody can see the birds flapping furiously in the breeze. She smiles.

Last month, the Burgoynes won a weekend stay in the motel where Melody sometimes relaxes with a $4 swim. While raffle tickets were being drawn in St. Anthony's Church, two of the Balcombs nearly died in the parking lot siphoning gas from a Chevy Caprice with plates that said: Have a Nice Day, Somewhere Else. The minister found them, hoses in their mouths, with old Mrs. Balcomb yelling, "It was the potato salad that made 'em sick. I don't never trust it."

The father is limping and sucking in wind as if he's finishing off a milkshake. *Wiiihhhhhhh*. He has a stutter of a blond beard and a faint tattoo on one flabby bicep. *Billy*, it says, by way of introduction. Billy leads his son, who is wearing a bathing suit with a built-in flotation device that Melody can see on a CBC consumer show. The boy's face is so gaunt that his eyes look gigantic, the plate-shaped eyes of black velvet mall art, a kitschy portrait from Tijuana.

The mother, named Carinna, pulls up a chaise lounge and rests. Melody smiles again. When Melody's father was dying, too ill to lift his paintbrush, Carinna came to the door with fresh-baked rolls. Melody's father touched her ruddy face and whispered, "Botticelli."

Wiihhhh. Billy waddles by in a Budweiser tank top and shorts. He weighs about two eighty; three toes are missing from one fat foot. His battered Vega is filled with

Crispy Crunch wrappers, Tim's cups and chip bags, which he explains to anyone who notices with, "I takes my meals in my car." Billy's eyes narrow, he seems confused as though he's someplace strange: a French restaurant or an underground garage. *Wiihhhh*—he sucks in wind—*wiihhhh*—and suddenly, feeling the need to do something, to act before the strangeness consumes him, Billy hurls the boy into the pool.

Craaaackkkk. Melody flinches as the head hits concrete.

"Caarinna." Billy ignores the crack and shouts to his wife as though they are the only people for miles.

"Caarinnnnnnnnnnaaaaaaa." It is a high reedy voice that creaks from need. *Wiiihhhhhhhh*. "Look, look!" The boy is sputtering, but Billy is calling Carinna. Billy's flesh-engulfed eyes have a puzzled innocence, distant and whimsical, permanently fixed on duelling go-karts and winterized fishing camps. His open mouth shows missing teeth. "Look, look," His voice is cracking with misplaced pride, and in a flash Melody can imagine him doing something horrible, like slicing off his son's foot with a ride-on mower, and crying the most awful endless tears.

The email beeps, another message.

> Ralph Klein should look at guys like Buckaroo before he starts slamming Maritimers. Klein couldn't clean Buckaroo's boots.

Merle makes his way to Elizabeth's desk, which is deep in birdwatching books and the tomes of poetry she wades through at night, wrestling with the cosmic, angelic and eternal damnation. Elizabeth is weeping over a photo of a couple in a cabin cruiser. *Mike and Bobby Toast 11 Years of Unwedded Bliss*. Mike looks like a guy who poaches lobsters and ransacks cottages for beer.

Merle remembers when Elizabeth had a short story—something about a train station—published in a literary journal, then wasted it all on Gordie Campbell, a hard-drinking city editor who played her until she was faded and cross, until he retired to a Florida condo with his lovely wife, Gail. Merle hands Elizabeth a tissue, which she uses to wipe her eyes. Melody thinks about Billy and Merle, she thinks about chances never had, and chances squandered.

*

For an exceptional cat, Georgie enjoyed simple pleasures like his daily drive. At midnight, when the streets were asleep, Melody fired up her gas-powered scooter. Capable of thirty miles per hour, the scooter was purple with a black base.

Georgie rode in a Snugli, craning his neck in the night air, closing his gold eyes in rapture. "For my money," Melody confessed, "there is nothing more splendid than the face of a cat, ears back, eyes closed, smiling."

For safety, they drove on the sidewalk, and at top speed Melody was vigilant to avoid overhanging branches or cracks in the cement or, occasionally, shift workers. One night, they were trailed by drunks from a bar, who followed them in a Jeep, shouting, "Scooter girl. Scoot this." Contemplative, Georgie ignored them, even when the drunks slammed into a parked minivan, causing an explosion of glass and chrome.

*

Melody believes everyone should keep a list of things that are important about them. She has hers:

1. She once had a cat named Georgie, who had links to the dark side, paranormal powers that could drive you insane.
2. She knew the Dance of the Moths.
3. Her favourite word was marsupial.
4. She had a foster child in Brazil who could draw perfect horses.

Before he was abducted, Georgie predicted that the world would end in a giant slumber and everyone would awake wearing gold slippers and scarlet serapes. There would be unicorns and talking cats and gauzy yellow sheers that let in a hue of healing. Everyone would know how to swim, ride bareback, and recreate the Pantheon by Etch a Sketch. There would be no starting line, no runningrunningrunning to catch up.

Strange Girls

In front of Jimmy was the Frankfurter family.

The father was a thug who jostled shoppers in the deli department and pressed too close to seniors at the school Christmas pageant. "Hey grandma," he sneered one year, pointing at a stalled walker. "What part of *walk* do you not understand?"

Like an outbreak of lice, Frank's mere presence made people uneasy. He showed up at parent-teacher night in too-tight sweats, *Anna Karenina* symbolically clutched in one hand. "I'm into more cerebral pursuits these days," he said, without provocation or room for reasonable response. "I'm an intellectual."

Despite his intellectual facade, Frank had enrolled his eight-year-old in an intense weightlifting program involving free weights and pulleys. When Tobin was cut during hockey tryouts, the mother howled in protest, the sight of an isometric lat pull fresh in her mind. "He's a powerhouse," she wailed. "A powerhouse."

Traumatized by his hockey failure and his mother's overwrought reaction, Tobin, one day during lunch, toppled six desks, spilling crayons, notebooks and action figures of Kobe and Shaq. The outburst came during the bullying hysteria sweeping the country like McCarthyism, urging youngsters to step up and name names. Tobin had acted out, the mother claimed, because *he* had been bullied, and when two suspects were summoned to the principal's office like commie screenwriters, Tobin stood in the hall and mooned them.

Mooning was the trademark of Thad, the Frankfurter golden boy, who stripped hood ornaments from neighbouhood cars.

The Frankfurters pushed small girls off bicycles, sent anonymous threats to coaches, yet tonight they sat before Jimmy, spellbound and humbled, at *The Passion of the Christ*. Mr. Frankfurter was eating a supersized popcorn soaked with hydrogenated butter-flavoured fat and he wore the pained face of a man in tight pants. As blood dripped from Christ's hand, Tobin sobbed hysterically, then gazed at his father for approval, as though this outburst might somehow compensate for his hockey failure.

Lips glistening with fat, Frank nodded back.

*

Frank Frankfurter was a school guidance counsellor, his wife, Liz, a social worker, details that had left the neighbourhood in a state of cognitive dissonance when revealed months after their arrival. The only consolation to Jimmy was that the Frankfurters were short and squat, which seemed certain to genetically derail Mr. Frankfurter's dreams of the NHL and ensure endless jokes about their suggestive surname.

"It comes from the city in Germany," Tobin would say.

"No," his tormenters would shout. "It comes from a pig."

*

It had been snowing for three days and the plow driver had blocked them in again. The driver had taken all the snow from a nearby cul-de-sac and left it in Jimmy's driveway.

This was a setback for Jimmy, charged with shovelling at home and working two nights a week at the movie theatre. Despite an epidemic of blizzards, Jimmy's father, Les, refused to buy a slow blower because the machines were, unbeknownst to Toro, "unnecessary polluters and capitalist tools." Les was the kind of man who used words like "funky" and "Trotskyite," but rarely in the same sentence. He also had a bad back, which precluded shovelling.

From his snowed-in driveway, Jimmy could see the stunted form of Thad Frankfurter pushing a snow blower with 8.5 horsepower and an electric starter. Living near the Frankfurters was, Jimmy believed, like being a sheep in a canyon ringed by coyotes. Motorized to the max, the family owned two ATVs, a powerboat, and a go-kart that Tobin drove like a maniac, once hitting a Shih Tzu named Li Ming.

Jimmy slouched in Les's Volvo, disappointed school had not been cancelled. Besides the sixty-centimetre snowfall, students had been subjected to a Code Three lockdown after teachers found a gun inside a locker.

Jimmy scraped his window with a thumbnail, creating ice curls. Yesterday, the gym teacher, in a desultory attempt to embrace the elements, had moved the class outdoors. Gamely, the teacher had strapped on the school's only equipment, a pair of antique snowshoes, waterlogged and weighing ten kilograms. As he stumbled and sank into banks, underdressed students slid down a hill on garbage bags and empty pizza boxes stained with oil and cheese.

The outside was a vacuum, devoid of life and warmth, with nothing to spark Jimmy's brain cells. Winter in Nova

Scotia was like being on a failed camping trip: the novelty quickly passed, leaving you cold and damp, fighting the collective will of nature.

Jimmy watched pedestrians trip over ice bumps that had turned the sidewalk into a mogul run. He saw a boy with a clarinet skirt two hoods, dressed in white, intimidators who stood at the end of a hallway, daring students to enter. He slouched lower as he saw a familiar pack of girls, poseurs who claimed as their icons Peter Pan and Hello Kitty.

Two of the Strange Girls were in his chemistry lab which, last week, had ended traumatically when someone spilled a bottle of hydrochloric acid and Mr. Sharma, following procedure, ordered three students into the safety shower, naked. When one boy balked, Mr. Sharma began screaming, "Code Two! Code Two!" and ordered everyone to flee.

The Strange Girls mocked classmates who were "shallow" enough to wear makeup or iron their hair, but they wrote long, jerk-off journal entries to an A-hole named Craig, who tormented a girl in Jimmy's class because she was a gymnast.

"Look at your man arms," taunted Craig, who favoured AC/DC t-shirts. "You dyke."

"Shut up, Craig, you motard."

"Man arms."

The Strange Girls, who collected unicorns and fairy motifs, snickered. Jimmy knew he was luckier than the gymnast, being, for the most part, as invisible as a cafeteria worker, the non-person who cleared tables, ignored by band geeks, dopers and the gangstas who wore white ball caps, brims raised skyward like an F-U, and wiped their brows of imaginary sweat.

When not performing oral sex on the despicable Craig, the Strange Girls gushed about improv or busking. *Who's your favourite Sailor Moon character?* Jimmy overheard them make dates to go sledding or comb the city for the perfect playground slide. Wearing used clothes, they courted the middle-aged English teacher by proclaiming a love for Woody Guthrie and the Grateful Dead. They were, Jimmy believed, psychotically precious.

Jimmy's father pulled ahead, then back, trying to see around a snowbank that had turned the intersection into a game of Russian roulette. Jimmy held his breath. The elements were pushing with more force than one human could resist, one sapped individual with the air sucked from his being.

Despite the snow, a Strange Girl was wearing nylon fairy wings.

"What an idiot," Jimmy muttered, glaring at the pink wings.

"Jimmy," his father scolded. "Why would you criticize someone for expressing herself? Just because she doesn't dress in Gap."

"You don't understand."

"I understand that I don't want you to be one of those nasty boys who thinks he's better than everyone."

Les was like a man in a foreign country; he didn't speak the language or understand the cultural signposts. It was all about nuance and irony and saying one thing while meaning another. Trucker hats meant urban camp, the poor old Boston Celtics, heroes of working-class Irish, had become as gangsta as do-rags and tatts, hippie meant outcast, and a big fat x on your hand meant that you were high on E, but pretending to be straight-edge. Hockey players wrestled in the showers but laughed at the effeminate dancer named Marcel who secretly met an older man in an apartment, then confessed about it on his blog. If he had trouble sorting it out, Jimmy sighed, how could Les, a man who listened to Jackson Browne, possibly understand? Still, he had bigger things to worry about.

*

Jimmy saw a truck filled with men in stocking caps and orange vests. Shorty's Landscaping. The truck had shovels and snow blowers and appeared headed to a restaurant parking lot, or if Jimmy closed his eyes and dreamed, *his* house. Snow blowers started at three hundred bucks for the flimsy electric model. Shorty's had Pro Jobs, bigger than anything the Frankfurters owned, snow eaters, sick and stoked.

Jimmy rubbed a purple bruise, just above his hip bone.

*

Jimmy's father had named him Fergus after a Scottish ancestor, but at the age of eight, Jimmy had insisted on using his second name, James.

When Les turned fifty, instead of celebrating with a cruise or party, he made a donation to African orphans. While Jimmy's father had become more earnest, his mother had moved in the opposite direction. Something had happened to Giselle, Jimmy observed, some type of hormonal imbalance that had left her in a state of permanent merriment. While other menopausal mothers had become depressed and reclusive, Giselle had turned giddy.

"Do you think you should see a doctor?" asked Les.

"Why? So I can get Low-zac, instead of Prozac?"

Jimmy's family had a talking cat. A week after Gomez came to live in the house, Jimmy's mother started conversations with the animal. Before long, Giselle supplied Gomez's high-pitched cat voice and everyone, including Les, found themselves bantering with the animal, which had a pink nose like a pencil eraser. Gomez was kept indoors because he suffered from narcolepsy, which caused him to drop without warning to the ground and snooze, even in traffic.

Les walked to work which gave him time to sort through his thoughts. It was time well spent, Jimmy believed. Les was the world's worst storyteller. Whenever he sensed he was losing his audience through tedium, when the banal nature of his account had become clear, he sped up, refusing to stop and, therefore, surrender the floor. A panic talker, he kept going when a rational person might quit.

Giselle, on the other hand, was succinct. Since her transformation, she had also become a gourmand, cooking and eating a multitude of fine foods. Matthew, Jimmy's ten-year-old brother, had joined her and now weighed a robust one hundred and twenty pounds, almost as much as Jimmy.

Matthew spent his spare time writing companies on the Internet, praising their products and requesting stickers. Posing as a bike enthusiast, he told one firm he was enjoying their four-thousand-dollar bike shocks. "The snowboard carved well in powder," he informed another. The creatine-laced energy drink was energizing.

One day, Matthew showed Jimmy two shoeboxes full of stickers, perfect for water bottles, skateboards or walls. That afternoon, a package arrived with twenty-eight dollars postage containing swimming pool plans, sample tiles and a how-to video.

✳

Jimmy and his father went into a music store.

"Oh look," Les murmured, "there's Stephen," a neighbour from two doors down.

It was clear that Stephen had undergone an extreme make-over that had started with his hair, dyed black and cut into bangs. Matching the hair were black-rimmed glasses although, as far as anyone knew, Stephen had perfect vision. Stephen wore tight slacks. On his feet were heavy shoes with rubber soles, and he carried himself like a spectral, albeit dark-haired, Andy Warhol.

It was a marked change from last year, which saw Stephen dressed in Roots and jeans. As Jimmy and his father approached the counter with a Carlos Santana disc, the transformed Stephen turned his head.

"Stephen snubbed us," Les reported back home, shocked.

"Dad, he's always like that now," Jimmy explained.

"You two used to play together."

"He's emo, Dad, he's emo."

"What the hell is emo?"

Jimmy sighed, close to tears. "It's short for emotional and they all follow the same type of music."

"That doesn't mean he can't speak to people."

Later that day, Giselle visited the store, where the emo clerks were so cool that icicles had formed on the counter. The Get Up Kids slouched on a wall. Giselle was accompanied by Matthew, who, going through a strange stage of his own, was wearing a ZZ Top T-shirt. They had treated themselves to a Japanese meal and had small but matching stains on their pants.

All around them, moody clerks were wearing tight pants, polyester button-up shirts, glasses and chunky black shoes. All were deathly thin and some appeared, upon close inspection, to be wearing hair barrettes and makeup.

"Oh," Giselle said in a stage voice, ostensibly directed at Matthew. "I don't see Stephen. He said he'd be working." A clerk snuck a peek through his heavy glasses. Stephen knew *these two?*

Giselle moved to the back, near another employee in a gas station jacket, leaning over the Dashboard Confessional CDs. "Stephen said he'd be here. I hope he didn't have to go to *court* again."

Outside, they laughed.

Jimmy dodged Stephen for a day, then said screw it. He had bigger things to worry about.

Giselle had become obsessed with *Manhunt,* the search for America's most gorgeous male model. The program had already aired in the States so she knew the winner, a hunk named Jon. The episodes appeared at random times, midnight or five p.m., with the same one—the cross-dressing show—popping up repeatedly. On the website, she said, the discussion board kept returning to which of the models were gay. Three were out, breathless viewers alleged, with at least another suspect.

Les made a show of leaving the room whenever *Manhunt* aired, claiming to be offended by the exploitative nature of the show. Jimmy tried to ignore him.

"Are they all gay?" asked Matthew.

"No," said Giselle, transfixed. "Just four." She squinted at the screen. "Well, maybe five."

Manhunt was one of many useless topics Jimmy's parents debated. For the life of him, Les couldn't understand reality TV, punk music or skateboard shoes, especially when sensible Mountain Equipment Co-op footwear was available. "I've been a member since 1973 when I bought my first backcountry gear."

"Lighten up, Les," urged Giselle.

Les was also concerned about the death of Susan Sontag, while Giselle, who found the writer sanctimonious, was less perturbed. "I think Gore Vidal had it right when he said Sontag's intelligence exceeded her talent."

What, Jimmy wondered, were they talking about? Every time Jimmy turned on the TV, a blizzard warning crawled across the screen like a death sentence, causing his chest to tighten. What if he couldn't handle it all? Snow blowers, Les declared, were partly to blame because they contributed to global warming, skewing the weather.

Shift workers were immune to winter, Jimmy figured, because their world was still and shut down. They were always in the survival mode of a frog, buried in mud at the bottom of a lake. Invisible, inconsequential, free even of the need for polite conversation.

Taxis raced across the bridge at four a.m. and, out of habit, rode your bumper even though they had nowhere to go. Clerks at the twenty-four-hour grocery stocked shelves while insomniacs roamed.

Jimmy told Les he was thinking of becoming a taxi driver, working the night run from the airport.

"I don't think that's a good idea."

"Why not?"

Les paused, looking for safe political ground. "Maybe you should see the guidance counsellor."

"The guidance counsellor?"

"Yes, isn't that what they're there for?"

Jimmy sighed. Frank Frankfurter's office was visited only by those who had lost their free will: society's sinners, the group-home pariahs and daycare mothers, who deposited their screaming babies in a classroom, then slept. Overnight, he noticed, the snow had hardened like cement blocks that could not be penetrated with a shovel and would stand there, part of the landscape, until spring.

*

It had seemed like a good idea. Jimmy had borrowed Les's credit card, then given it to Matthew, who had, through the Internet, ordered a snow blower.

It wasn't just any piece of crap, they determined. The $2,499.00 Pro Job, king of snow blowers, came with a thirteen-horsepower engine for extra muscle and a twelve-volt key battery. The PJ had hand warmers, a headlight and heavy-duty skid shoes. With a throwing distance of twenty metres, it weighed a manly seventy kilograms. According to the online information, the PJ came with eight speeds and a cast-iron gear case. Delivery was free.

The plan was to use the snow blower briefly, until Jimmy could get a handle on the buildup, then return it. It had to work, Jimmy figured, or he wouldn't make it.

February was bad, but it was only the start.

Could anything be as bleak as snowplows in April, freezing rain and dark, lifeless windows? Flabby people who could barely muster the strength to move — people who had bravely fought through December, January, even February, bundling up for walks, traipsing through snowbanks and slush, smiling at Christmas lights and heading into rinks for family skates. By April, they were cooked. Defeated. "What made you think you could make it?"

Winter laughed in their faces. "What made you think I was done?" Jimmy couldn't face that alone.

*

"What if you lived in Switzerland?" asked Les nonsensically. This wasn't Switzerland, Jimmy groaned, where trains ran from towns to ski hills, where chalets served hot chocolate and pastry. This was an apocalypse of clogged streets, frayed nerves and shivering teens in Columbia jackets and sneakers sliding down hills on pizza boxes.

*

For thirty years, Giselle had been trapped in Grade Eight, the ugly year that saw her sprout four inches, gain twenty pounds, and try, without luck, to straighten her curly hair. Haunting her was a lumpy girl with pressed bangs, a creature so hideous that Giselle had poked out her face in the junior-high yearbook Jimmy found in a drawer.

Nothing fit. One day, in desperation, Giselle wore her mother's dress to school, a purple wrap, and heard, to her mortification, snickers. They came from Mrs. Skankle, the math teacher, a shrew who wore tight skirts and matching sweaters. Shiny high heels she liked to click click.

"You are going to be a messy old woman," Skankle told her, while examining a jumbled page of fractions, and Giselle knew, from the tone, that the insult extended past the page. In teenage stories, the girls are always awkwardly taller than the boys, but that wasn't the issue. It would have been okay if Giselle had been a five-foot-eight swan who glided through halls, but she was lumpy and round, too hormonally altered for that androgynous age.

Les had never endured that. He was the indistinguishable teen, the unworthy target, average in every way, a balsam fir in the forest. It had taken a menopausal mix-up, a hormonal rearrangement of mysterious scope, for Giselle to reach a sanguine state. All of this she wanted to tell Jimmy, but didn't.

"Just keep the bloody thing," Jimmy heard her say instead. "Life doesn't have to be about deprivation, Les. You can live a little."

"That's what's wrong with families today," Les sputtered. "Everyone is living in the moment, wearing stupid clothes, like that Stephen, and listening to music that shouldn't even be called music."

"For God's sake, Les, when we were young, radio stations played 'My Ding-a-ling'. How can you laugh at goths and punks when you had snoop boots and an Apache scarf? You had platform shoes, Les, a dickey front."

Les stared, principles wasted on obsolete battles while enemies, new and insidious, had risen around him. In the hallway, Jimmy thought about how much he hated Craig, and going to school, and seeing the fat stupid face of Frank Frankfurter, who positioned himself at the entrance, near his empty office, and *accidentally* bumped you. As he bumped, Frankfurter managed to surreptitiously dig one elbow into your side and twist it so hard he left bruises, large purple blotches. Jimmy thought about tired arms and mountains of snow, and problems he just didn't need.

"It's not just fashion, Giselle. It's political values."

"I am tired of hearing about cool politicians from the seventies, Les. Pierre Trudeau, the paragon of cool, did Liona Boyd, for God's sake. Liona freakin' Boyd!"

"Ahhhhhhhhhh," Les sputtered, and Jimmy started to cry.

Moonbeam

I left home at four a.m., headed for the U.S. border. I was making good time until the road narrowed, trapping me behind a 1990 Grand Am held together with plastic filler and faith. The beater had six rosaries hanging from the rear-view mirror, and a vanity plate: REPENT.

As I pulled out to pass, I glanced at the driver, who looked as if he had been sprung from the federal prison in Renous. Bearded, he had paranoid eyes and skin the colour of wet cardboard. In the darkness, in an unmasked moment that sent a shiver up my neck, our eyes met, and, ignoring the tiny boy in the passenger seat, I nodded.

I met my wife at a sports celebrity dinner where I was transfixed by a female jockey with azure eyes. The eyes, which had been to a place of darkness and din, looked straight at me, I'm convinced, with a passion that felt like a heat lamp.

The jockey, Mary Boone, had been born in the Chicago projects, a circumstance that might have sealed her fate if not for a life-altering event. At age eight, Mary was struck by a bus and hurled into the air, shivering like a swordfish on the end of a line. In a coma for thirty days, she emerged with a look no one had seen before, a peaceful yet rapturous look, the look of a religious fanatic or an unstoppable Jeopardy winner.

"I'm going to race horses," she told her mother, bedside. While others sensed that Mary was different, too still, yet too tuned to inaudible sounds, Mary felt, for the first time, right. The reorganization of her brainwaves, the neuropsychological changes, enabled Mary to see beyond minutiae all the way to greatness. If she listened closely, the path would be clear.

Mary had her first race at a county fair with tractor pulls. "I was on a four-year-old filly named Jacki-O," she recalled. "I had dirt in my face and we finished fourth, but I'll never forget the rush."

On her way to countless rushes, Mary suffered a shattered pelvis that grounded her for six months but did nothing to dim her desire, nothing to silence the sounds. Bolted together with screws and nerve, Mary had her greatest win at the Belmont Stakes on a long shot named Moonbeam, a closer with large kind eyes. "In a race, it all comes down to one split-second decision: inside or out, go now or wait," said Mary, who had become, through mischance, a human beta blocker. "I waited and Moonbeam told me when."

When Delma phoned to ask me to lunch, I was galloping down a beach, arms around Mary Boone's waist. I barely remembered Delma, introduced by a colleague of mine at *The Bugle,* a goof who covered curling and lusted after elderly women.

Sometimes, when things are unbearable, I search for Mary's azure eyes; I imagine the smell of stables and sweat, the daring pursuit of dreams.

∗

I'm on my fourth coffee and my head has that displaced buzz, hovering on a cushion of caffeine. I hadn't planned on the fourth excessive cup until a near disaster.

After a snack at McDonald's, I was driving past snowmobile tracks and a gypsum mine when a massive creature came from nowhere and lunged at my car. All I saw were antlers, nostrils and a mammoth chest. Swerving, I avoided the creature, which I realized was a moose.

"Jesus!" I screamed, hitting gravel.

Why did the moose attack me, unprovoked? I wondered as I stared at the road so hard dots formed. Were others out there, waiting? In Newfoundland, I knew, there are five hundred collisions a year with moose, drawn to pavement by salt and roadside vegetation. But this didn't seem like a collision, it was an attack, a telekinetic intervention by Delma to keep me from reaching my salvation. My cellphone rings but I will not answer. Probably her.

Delma Heywood is a TV commentator and a columnist at the rival *News*. Her face is on billboards, chin cocked at a pugilistic angle like Joey Buttafucco.

Delma is short with a large, made-for-TV head. She wears tight skirts and altitudinal heels that make it impossible for her to walk like a human. Her top half does not move and her legs stick straight out, unbending, struggling for balance. She moves with the grace of one of those huge beasts at a container pier, those towering four-legged cranes that look as though they escaped from Star Wars and could, at any time, topple.

Delma is as subtle as a sledgehammer and almost as thick. She thinks "Somalis" are a Mexican dish, a "misogynist" a person who works on sore backs. At parties, she uses the word "vagina" repeatedly, either for shock value, or simply to show she knows the word.

I wish I could say I love my wife. I wish she made me feel as alive and dauntless as Mary Boone, who coaxed her mounts to victory with whispers, not a whip. I married Delma because I couldn't say no, because I was afraid she might think I didn't love her because I was weak, when in fact, I didn't love her because she is as mean and dangerous as the homicidal moose.

※

Last week, I covered a AAA hockey game.

Despite the protests of Hockey Canada, which disingenuously says, "It is just a game," minor hockey is a caste system. It starts with the untouchables in house league and ascends to AAA, the highest caste, which gratuitously affixes its three magic letters to every garment. Only from AAA can you see the apoplectic face of Don Cherry.

The rink was full of parents, groupies and hockey nuts who chuckled when the organist played "Three Blind Mice." Next to me sat a chubby girl, who kept tilting her head back and dropping fries into her mouth like a keeper feeding a dolphin.

Near the players' bench, I spotted Eddie Winchell, a columnist from *Hockey Monthly,* eating a hot dog. Winchell, who got his start at a local paper, had become insufferable, phoning acquaintances from exotic locations and gloating, "I'm on a plane to Moscow. Excuse me while I say hello to Marcus."

I noticed Winchell watching number 48, a fast-moving forward. The kid was small, I figured, but had that extra something, the indescribable It.

He was the son of a guy who used to work at my paper. I'd often see them at games and Jack, the dad, was always pleasant, hoping I would do something on the kid, but never bold enough to ask. This was a man who got up at four a.m. to drive to a rink, who ran bottle drives, who wore outdated clothes, all to chase a dream he and the boy seemed dangerously close to achieving. Why would I help him? Jack was too content, too pleased with the life he'd managed to eke out, too bloody proud of the boy. I could see it in his face and it made me feel small and mean and absolutely bitter.

The home team won 6–4 and Jack's boy scored twice. I smiled at my former colleague, just enough to make him optimistic.

"Your boy had a good game."

"Not too shabby." Jack tried not to look excited.

"See ya."

Instead of feeling shame, I felt power over Jack, who had made himself vulnerable by building a life on the flimsy foundation of hope. I thought about Oscar Wilde, who, when headed to trial, learned the opposing lawyer was a former classmate from Oxford. "No doubt," Wilde quipped, landing on a sad human truth, "he will pursue his case with the added bitterness of an old friend."

Before I met Delma, I would have written about Jack's boy and I would have done a damn fine job. I won a National Newspaper Award for my profile of a crippled skier, who now teaches handicapped children and races, every night, down the same magnificent hill. I did a feature on an arm wrestler and mother of five. Instead of writing about athletes with hearts as big as California, I now write about conflict of interest and misappropriation. I spent months doing a series on eligibility in university sports. It won an award, and a hoop star from Georgia, a lanky guard with two kids back home, got the boot.

This is all Delma's fault. She was born aggrieved, I discovered after our marriage; everyone had wronged her: men, schools, social workers. Conscripted, I became an unwilling soldier in her never-ending war.

Delma, Delma, Delma. I didn't want to marry Delma. I

didn't even want to date her. I was a tidy man who could lose myself in linescores, race through agate like a spy thriller. I liked jazz CDS, model trains, Elmore Leonard books. I liked bold, brassy people from a circumspect distance. At times, I thought I might be gay, but I didn't even care.

*

I get stopped for speeding near the border. I try to explain the moose attack and the subsequent coffee, but it just doesn't fly. The officer reminds me of my cousin, Carl, who used to run a lumber business.

Carl was plump and always referred to himself as a porker, which he found hilarious. He and his wife lived outside town, the picture of contentment with snowmobiles, ATVs and a backyard trampoline. Then, for some reason, Carl, the porker, had an affair with his bookkeeper, a betrayal discovered by his wife.

The last time I saw Carl, he looked like a man who had suffered a minor head injury.

He was driving a rundown taxi and seemed desperate to tell me about his life.

"I'm married to a native woman," said Carl, a greasy ponytail down his back.

"Okay, that's great."

Carl looked at me too hard, looking for a reaction I didn't have, expecting me, I assume, to judge his philandering ways and low-paying job. "When she retires, we're going to move to native land." What did he want from me? Forgiveness, guidance? "You have to get used to living with natives," he added without encouragement. "They have a different concept of time. Six o'clock supper doesn't mean six for them."

I take my ticket and continue, ignoring my ringing cellphone.

＊

Last month, a tree hugger phoned our house. He was trying to stop a condo development Delma had endorsed. When Delma held the phone away from her ear, I heard the hugger quoting an Eastern proverb about shouted lies and whispered truths. I covered my ears, avoiding her shouted response, "*How* did you get my home number?"

Delma's column landed in thousands of homes, the hugger was smeared by unnamed sources, the *News* trashed six letters to the editor, but don't, don't you *dare* call Delma at home. The hugger knows his options are limited. Delma has never heard of Oscar Wilde and Lord Alfred Douglas and their sordid tale of sodomy and revenge, but the rest of us know, from that historic lesson, that it is rarely wise to sue.

When I first saw Delma's meanness, I made allowances for her humble upbringing. Her father was a truck driver and her mother cleaned office towers at night. One tower was owned by the *News* publisher, who decided, in return for years of meticulous cleaning, to give the daughter a job.

"What does she like to do, Millie?" he asked.

"She wanted to be a veterinary assistant but that didn't work out so she got a job at a car dealer's."

"All right, we'll put her in the newsroom."

Delma started on the police beat, but after a harrowing clash with bikers, went on stress leave. Unfit for regular duty, she was inexplicably promoted to columnist. It was a throwaway position and better than paying long-term leave. Her columns were usually ignored, occasionally mocked by the chi-chi crowd. Nonetheless, she found a niche as a small-c conservative and Board of Trade darling.

The CBC hired her as a commentator to balance a rabid immigration lawyer who ran for the Marxist-Leninists and staged sit-ins at points of departure. It was a smug little joke on the right that slowly, over time, backfired. Delma bought yellow suits. She had her teeth capped, her hair highlighted by a Hungarian named Attilla. The newspaper ran photos of Delma looking combative and the CBC, outsmarted at its own game, renewed her contract. For the Marxist lawyer, it was like playing tennis with a hacker. Over time, his game became pointless, dulled by chasing directionless balls and stupefying non sequiturs. Delma ascended.

*

Pulling into a greasy spoon, I park by a Neon with TASMANIAN DEVIL stencilled on the back window. The side windows are covered in stuffed animals attached with suction cups. Inside, I see one customer, an old woman in an eagle sweatshirt, who looks at me and scowls.

A waitress takes my order, then points to a sullen teen clearing tables. The tattooed teen loads plates into a rubber tub, clanking hard enough to break them.

"Don't pay no attention to him." She gestures again. "He's only here on accounta community service."

"Okay." It is clear that the teen is listening, growing more sullen.

"He don't even separate the recyclables. He's be more use to them in jail than he is to me." The teen scowls and she cocks her head at a defiant I-don't-care-if-he-hears-me angle. "If I stood on that overpass"— she points down the highway in the direction I'm heading —"and bifted a boulder onta someone's car, I'd be in jail. Me and my idiot friends."

Leaving the teen to his penance, I think about the day I married Delma in a courthouse at noon. It was a face-saving move for Delma, who had just been dumped by a digital media artist named Gino. Gino was part of the NFB scene and that rebuff fuelled Delma's disdain for the cool crowd, the hipsters, the pierced people who played with art and words, who quoted books and philosophers with foreign names. I met Gino years later and discovered he was cooler and better looking than I expected. Maybe he saw something in Delma I couldn't, I think, as I drive under the overpass. Suddenly, in a state of shock and apperception, I find myself clinging to the wheel, reeling from the impact of a boulder on my roof. Good God, I mutter, as I keep my eyes on the murderous highway.

✻

An hour ago, I checked into a motel in Albany, New York. Albany has the Pepsi Arena and Heritage Park, but most importantly, and the reason I planned my stopover here, it has the Saratoga Race Course.

After I met Mary Boone, I spent weeks immersed in thoroughbred racing. I became obsessed with Secretariat, who won the Belmont Stakes in 1973 by a surreal thirty-one lengths, eclipsing all records, sending a message from God as vivid as a parted sea. The Big Red Horse was so perfect, so explosive, that he bent the rules of bloodlines, and stood, in all his glory, above the machinations of man. What did it mean? I saw writers struggle to decipher the message, to describe the superhorse with superlatives and mythological references. It was daunting; Secretariat was more fantastic than Pegasus, who carried lightning bolts for Zeus, because he moved among us and seemed, at times, just a horse.

*

When I was eight, the same age as Mary Boone when she was hit by the bus, my class had a stuffed elephant. Everyone took Willy home, then recorded his activities in a journal. I had trouble with my l's, so I exaggerated them, letting them vibrate in my mouth until I knew they were there.

Willllllllllllllll-e, fat with a bow tie, went to Dairy Queen.

Willlll-e visited the wildlife park.

"So," my mother asked, "who took Willy home last night?"

"Maggie."

"What did they do?"

"They watched *Star Wars*."

"Whose turn is it tonight?"

"Willllllll-e won't be going home." I remember feeling odd. "He is going to Mrs. Graham's house for a bath."

"That's nice," my mother said, fishing in my bookbag.

> Dear Parents: I received a call from a parent from Mrs. Graham's class who notified me his son has lice. Please check your child's head and refer to the enclosed information. Mr. Bonter, Principal.

Our class had thirty students, including Simon, a Down's-syndrome boy, who had a sweet disposition but trouble with words. One day, Mrs. Sharp, the anorexic gym teacher, called Simon fat and made him cry. When word of Simon's sobbing spread, Mrs. Sharp told the principal *we* had bullied him. For some reason, the child-hater kept having kids, four in five years, all ignored by her husband, a compulsive runner, making her more angry, more sadistic with us.

After Willy's bath, Mrs. Sharp screened a video that showed six-legged insects crawling through small blond heads and sucking up blood. Actually the size of a sesame seed, the lice looked as large as hyenas. Small and blond, I was traumatized.

"Why would she show eight-year-olds that disgusting video?" demanded my sister after I woke up crying. "So they won't take up lice?"

"Don't talk about it," I whimpered.

"You know, lice are like crack," she continued sarcastically. "I'm in Grade Two, I think I'll try lice to be popular."

"*Don't talk about it!*"

"Stop!" my mother ordered, then mumbled, low enough to absolve herself of guilt: "She did it because she is an idiot who hates her own life." My sister smirked at Mom's lapse in behaviour and I felt more confused.

Last night, I saw myself rise in the dark and pick up a soapstone carving, a foot-tall bear a local bank had given Delma. The bear was curiously posed on its hind legs, head tilted back, arms raised awkwardly to the sky as if he was scaring off crows. I'd seen the pose before in Inuit carvings, but never the smile, which stretched across the bear's narrow face. Deliberately, and with the moral conviction of an Albanian driving a wooden stake through the heart of a vampire, I brought the bear down on Delma's head. Over and over. The harder I hit, the less impact the bear seemed to have, until finally Delma sat up and yawned, "Damn it, David, I have a column to write."

✶

Awakening in Louisville, I shower and dress in a white shirt and pants.

I wind down my window, half expecting to hear banjos and "Blue Moon of Kentucky." This is a state diverse enough to have produced Abe Lincoln and Muhammad Ali. It's the birthplace each year of nine thousand thoroughbreds, all with the same anniversary, January first, all bred by stables praying for the magical happenstance of the Big Red Horse.

It's the site of the Kentucky Derby, which epitomizes what I love about sports: the chance to defy the laws of nature, to do something life-affirming and grand. Like sex, it is all in the moment, when fear and abandon merge in a frisson of heat. You can replay footage of Roger Bannister's four-minute mile over and over and you can't get it. You had to be there to taste the endorphins and smell the pandemonium that erupted like fireworks, and landed, as sparks of inspiration, on obscure tracks half a world away.

I am going to find Mary Boone. I am going to see if she still rides with the nerves of a sniper and the soft touch of a fairy. I'd like to see a picture of Mary with the Belmont Stakes trophy, a tiffany silver bowl supported by three horses. I'd like to see a shot of Moonbeam, the underdog, draped in a blanket made of three hundred and fifty white carnations, imported from California or Bogota. Years after she rode her first mount at a fairground with llamas and giant pumpkins, I want to know if Mary still talks to horses. I want to see the world through azure eyes.

Eric Montross Sucks

MONDAY, TEN A.M.

Jeffrey's right leg twitches, then his left, like a pager set to vibrate. Sometimes, the twitches last for seconds, sometimes as long as *The Simpsons.*

"Mr. Maxwell got sent to jail for breaking the basketball net," he whispers.

"My mom said he's at another school," argues Brandon.

"No." Jeffrey is adamant. "Jail."

"Cool."

Mr. Maxwell used to be the Wood Point gym teacher, the only male educator other than Mr. Wheedle, the principal, rarely seen outside his office. Mr. Maxwell had played basketball in Europe; he had a tattoo on one shoulder: *Basketball Is Life*. He drove a greasy black Mustang and he wore hair gel and track pants open from ankle to knee. When Jeffrey had blood streaming from his ear—the result, later discovered, of a fingernail cut— Mr. Maxwell urged him to "shake it off, Jeffrey, shake it off."

Forsaken by the lusty Mr. Maxwell, who may or may not be incarcerated, Jeffrey is shackled to his desk and a puffer. He stares out the window at a static schoolyard, a soccer field of weeds. The only sound is the rumble of wheels on pavement as mothers haul toddlers by in rubber wagons. *Kalumph, kalumph,* a death march.

"Jeffrey!" Mrs. Joncas croaks. "Is that your cart in the hall?"

The Grade Six teacher looks as if she is staring down a pit of New York longshoremen, sweaty men with sharp hooks and larcenous intentions. Jeffrey focuses on Mrs. Joncas's stubby feet, stuffed in sandals, and thinks of giant frankfurters. He hears a clock tick.

Twitching, he rises to retrieve his Ready to Go, used on band days to transport his sax. Jeffrey hates the stupid cart, which old people use for groceries. Flimsy, it mires in mud, convulses in the wind like an inverted umbrella. Jeffrey floats to another place, a place with noise and movement. At an all-city concert last month, the Rocky Road boys balanced tubas on their hips, wore school hoop jackets and played the theme from *Mission: Impossible* as a daredevil, clad in black, slid down a zip line.

As Jeffrey returns to his seat, the despicable Holly hisses, "Wussss." In the stagnant room, he checks his pocket calendar: May twenty-ninth. Two more days.

Mr. Wheedle nods at the mall cop, then smiles at the lotto lady. He spots Bert, a mall walker, flushed from his aerobic outing.

"Anyone upstairs?" asks Bert in a hooded sweatshirt.

"Just Ed."

"Thanks for the warning."

In his Wood Point uniform, a short-sleeved shirt and wide tie, Mr. Wheedle leans over the railing to survey the entertainment court. What's new? Last week, there were model trains, a chow chow show. In one corner, half-hidden by artificial trees, he sees two women, stout and dogged as broomball players, in from the country.

Poker-faced, one marches across the lobby, which is festooned with fake spring flowers. Mr. Wheedle cranes his neck. A man takes the woman's money and pulls out an Afro comb, fluffing her perm, streaked with a grey bolt. There is a name for that. What is it? Grinning, the woman takes a series of square-dance steps, arms raised girlishly, until she lands in the lap of a pink and white Easter bunny. The bunny, wearing a bow tie and vest, has black eyes and a mouth that hangs open in a permanent guffaw, exposing a tongue and one huge tooth.

The man adjusts her legs.

The woman smiles for the camera.

She looks game, Mr. Wheedle decides, like a woman who would kick up her leg when she got a spare in bowling, drink green beer on St. Patrick's Day. She probably helps her husband run a trucking company, he figures, doing payroll.

The Easter bunny, petite enough to be a woman or a teen, remains mute, silenced either by the furry head or the protocol of being a bunny.

✻

> For the safety of our students, there will be No: monkey bars, Red Rover, touch football, four-square, scooters, bicycles, rollerblades, skateboards, marbles, skipping ropes, tiddlywinks, pixie sticks, or yo-yos.

"Russell won a staring contest with a cat," whispers Jeffrey.

"Yeah?" says Brandon, who has transparent skin and bones like chopsticks.

"I think the cat could have gone longer if he'd known it was a contest."

"Russell is a chump," Brandon declares and blinks in the sharp fluorescent lights. Brandon always looks downtrodden, as if it's the first day of school, turning his back on water fights and half-pipes. He has ponderous glasses that weigh him down and sap his will: old-man glasses, fixed and sated.

"I was in a staring contest with a Rottweiler," Jeffrey offers. "I went four hours and eight minutes."

"How come it's not in the *Guinness Book of Records*?"

"My mom forgot to send it in."

"Your mom is a chump."

Mrs. Joncas's classroom smells like the foot-products aisle at the drugstore. The walls are bare except for one chart and a bleached photo of the All-City Science Champs, pride of Wood Point, four prodigies with a homemade robot that picked up sticks. Whatever happened to the science club, Jeffrey wonders, the math fair? The date on the photo is as faded as Wood Point's brilliance: 1982.

"Look." Brandon nudges Jeffrey. In his fist is an edict from Mrs. Joncas that he crumples like an empty chip bag. Jeffrey laughs.

> Do you know a bully?
> If so, report him/her to the Office
> Bullying is
> gossiping
> exclusion
> using a loud voice
> not sharing
> making fun of someone
> bragging
> always winning games

B. J. Boutilier has reported Russell twice for wearing Adidas body spray, included in the ban on scents, nuts, mood rings, jelly bracelets and candy cigarettes. "Russell doesn't care," the boys boast with approbation when Mrs. Joncas's nemesis gets a detention.

On weekends, Russell, a recent émigré from Newfoundland, scales the roof for missing balls. He has blond hair that sticks out like the fur of a bathed cat. Under his T-shirt is a doughy stomach that shakes when he runs. He is sturdy as a circus bear. His brother is six two and it is clear that Russell is storing up fat for the surge that will make him as manly and dangerous as a cougar. At recess, he eats Cheezies and wipes his hands on his shirt. Yesterday, he offered Callum a drink from his bottle. The water, Callum discovered, was brown from the dirt around Russell's mouth. With bikes banned from the playground, Russell leaves his unattended, unlocked, one block away. "He doesn't care," the boys sigh with envy.

Jeffrey feels a flash of pain like a pinprick. Mr. Wheedle enters the classroom like the lead in a Cole Porter musical, grinning madly behind tinted glasses that darken outdoors and could, at any time, shatter from ebullience. "Hellloooo Grade Sixes."

Mr. Wheedle presides over eight classrooms, two hundred fifty students, twelve teachers and forty volunteers who roam the halls like zombies. The zombies are led by Mrs. Boutilier, B.J.'s environmentally-sensitive mother, who wears a grey bob and a homemade cape she brandishes like a whip. She is co-author, with Mrs. Joncas, of the school's stupendous list of rules. Mrs. Boutilier sniffs the grounds for violations, like Russell's bike, which she reports to Mr. Wheedle, who, on the slimmest pretense, escapes to the mall. When she passes boys in the hallway, she hugs the cape, protecting her bird-like frame, as though, in a hormone-crazed fit, they might jump her.

"I have reports of jaywalking...." The rest is lost on Jeffrey, who drifts to his yearbook entry, lifting his head sporadically to feign attention.

> NAME: Jeffrey Johnson
> BORN: Halifax
> FAVOURITE FOOD: Jumbo ribs
> HEIGHT: 134 cm, WEIGHT: 31 kilograms
> PETS: Iguana named Frank Grime
> HOBBY: Playing basketball, skateboarding
> FAVOURITE BAND: Limp Bizkit
> FAVOURITE SHOW: WWE Raw
>
> When I grow up I want to be an engineer who designs robots, shoes or cars. (Hummers, Lamborghinis and Porsches are my favourites. I like cars that are fast, tough, low to the ground and slick.)

*

TUESDAY, TEN A.M.

"Eric Montross sucks," Jeffrey whispers to Brandon, who dreams he is Shaq, riding an El Diablo custom hog built by Jesse James, badass proprietor of West Coast Choppers, owner of a Pay Up Sucker palm tattoo.

"What a waste of size," sneers Brandon.

"Two hundred and seventy pounds!"

"Montross is a chump."

Jeffrey watches the Primaries march by with sand buckets, led by the merry Miss Willoughby, who is as odd and exotic a tulip in winter. The Primaries live on a separate planet, one floor away, near a storeroom of shelved microscopes and rocket launchers that could, just could, go off at any minute. One day, Mrs. Joncas sent Jeffrey to the storeroom with an outdated globe. Inside, he found an illuminated solar system and handmade models of strange-looking animals. Evolutionary Stages of the Horse (family Equidae), said the label. The smallest animal, which Jeffrey held up to the light, looked like a fox with five separate toes. The largest, Jeffrey noted, had solid hooves and long skinny legs for speed.

Jeffrey tightens his watch, hanging like a shackle.

Brandon's mother says Mr. Maxwell is teaching at Calvin Webster, where the boys wear baby blue ball caps. They have track suits and flame-covered short sets like summer pyjamas. Do-rags. Teeth they cover up. Instead of band, they take leadership, which consists of wrestling and bowling. They follow girls lasciviously with their eyes until the girls flinch or giggle. They wear earrings and cornrows. They chew tobacco, which comes in flavours like raspberry and can make you hurl.

Jeffrey hopes Brandon's mother is wrong, that Mr. Maxwell really *is* in jail, pumping iron until his biceps turn into bowling balls, planning his return. Mr. Maxwell's replacement wears orthopaedic shoes; she doles out skipping and calisthenics. Last week, while driving home, she froze on the bridge, panic-stricken, as horns honked behind her. A victim of its homogeneous neighbourhood and once-stellar standards, Wood Point has become a haven for dilapidated teachers, too frail for Ritalin and knives, too worn to rise up against Mrs. Boutilier's misguided army.

Kalumph, kalumph.

✷

WEDNESDAY, TEN A.M.

"Jeffrey!" Mrs. Joncas's eyes are enormous orbs trapped

by dense sweaty glasses. They remind Jeffrey of bloated goldfish, too fat and desperate for their ten-gallon tank, exploding goldfish with bladder problems.

"Huh?"

"It's your turn." Mrs. Joncas points to the chart, and Jeffrey numbly rises. Oh, crap: the thirty-first.

She slides a ruler into the wall, skimming Jeffrey's hair. One hundred and thirty centimetres.

She burps approval.

Wheezing, Jeffrey studies his graph that is now four centimetres *below* August, when Montross mercifully retired from the NBA. Jeffrey sighs as though he's been saddled with the inept seven-foot centre for another year. He pulls out his calculator for the U.S. conversion, the NBA equivalent: four foot two.

Kalumph, kalumph.

"Brandon."

One hundred and thirty-nine centimeters. Jeffrey's shrinking leg twitches.

Jeffrey scrutinizes Brandon's chart. All of the boys, deprived of hormones and movement, have shrunk, all except Russell, who somehow, subversively, has grown as large as Holly, who lurks outside Brandon's house like a bounty hunter, tracking her prey before he vanishes like vapour. B. J. Boutilier is under four feet tall. Mrs. Joncas records the cumulative loss: one hundred and twenty-two centimetres, almost one full boy.

"Excellent!"

Jeffrey stares at a closet full of Ready to Go's and one steel-framed cart with a bearing capacity of three hundred pounds. He takes a puffer hit. Mrs. Joncas burps again, and Jeffrey strains to hear the Primaries singing in their upstairs oasis.

*"Our work is done, it's time to sa-ay
Goodbye until another da-ay."*

The Grade Six boys had left Miss Willoughby, who lived in a land of tooth fairies and talking bears, but they recalled her kindness and knew she had not abandoned them, just preserved them, in her mind, as toothless tykes who clung to legs. Jeffrey leans towards Brandon, who may be crying behind his ponderous glasses.

"Remember that day," whispers Jeffrey, "when Mr. Maxwell came down the court and pointed his finger at B. J. and said, 'get out of my house' and B. J. cried."

Brandon sniffles. "He spun up and slammed."

"He smashed the net."

"B. J. told Mrs. Joncas."

"B. J. is a chump."

*

WEDNESDAY, TWO P.M.

Mr. Wheedle ignores his cell. It is probably Mrs. Boutilier, complaining about a car parked near the school. Who, she'd want to know, owns a Chevy Impala with a VISA sticker on the window? Or it could be about Russell. Did you know, she would shriek, eyes bouncing like pinballs, that Mrs. Wrobleski saw Russell purchasing fireworks at that native reserve?

Like many of the volunteers, driven over the brink by compulsive lawn maintenance, indifferent husbands and truncated dreams, Mrs. Boutilier is on medication, operating in a manic mode you cannot penetrate. When Mr. Wheedle came to Wood Point, he thought she was lively, an ambitious conversationalist, and then he realized she was bombed. Blasted. And now she is phoning his cell reporting jaywalkers and organizing petitions and she cannot be stopped, this cyclone of pharmaceutically induced energy, this hurtling force of supermomdom resurrected from a bed of depression and angst, unleashed on *him*.

Mr. Wheedle nods at the mall cop.

The cop nods back.

Mr. Wheedle closes his eyes and sees Maria, tall and blonde and winsome. Scrubbed, she smells like lemon, the perpetual crack of dawn. Her skin is unmarked, and when he touches it gingerly, in a state of automation, it feels as soft as unbaked rolls. Maria, Maria. Just eighteen, lead in the high school production of *The Tempest*, lovely as wildflowers, even with a pierced brow. Mr. Wheedle thinks about his old school, his reckless fall. He thinks about how tiny and pale the boys have become. Castrated by innuendo, he walks the halls a sinner, stripped of moral outrage, the strength to act. Mr. Do-Nothing, they call him. *They* know. *He* knows. Mr. Wheedle tries to forget when he lies in his sinner's bed, and in his one act of defiance, feels Maria's skin, hears her laugh and smells the unmistakable scent of lemon.

He sees the bunny, head tucked under one arm like a motorcycle helmet. At the bus stop, smoking. He looks twenty-five, with a lightning bolt scar on his cheek. He is still in the furry body and, unlike Clarence the Christmas Elf, makes no attempt to hide the fraud.

His eyes, which Mr. Wheedle assumed were red and non-seeing, are jaded and cross as a lynch mob.

"Need a lift?" asks Mr. Wheedle behind the darkened glasses.

"Sure," says the bunny, hoisting the head.

One Bad Bounce

They called him Bouncy.

Before school each day, while kids were clustered like grapes, gossiping, fretting over hair, Bouncy stood in a ring with his friends, all half his size. Bouncy was five eight, one ninety, hefty for Grade Seven. His friends were prepubescent mites.

Without warning, the mites would attack Bouncy, hurl themselves at him, and he would bounce them through the air with his corpulent belly. Sometimes, they attacked in pairs, and Bouncy would have to pivot for the second bounce. After twenty minutes, Bouncy never seemed tired, just winded.

No one cared since Bouncy was from the poor side of town and his clothes were shabby and plaid as if he had elderly parents on social assistance. He had clown hair, aviator glasses from Costco. The high-voiced mites were nameless, as inconsequential as dust.

One day, after an exceptional attack, Owen bounced through the air like a miss-hit tennis ball, a hurtling mass of kinetic energy, sailing past a tree straight onto a rock. It was as though someone had stored Owen in a freezer, rearranging his molecular structure for one stupendous bounce. Ooohhhhh! The cool girls slithered over for a peek. The principal descended. While Owen lay motionless in a Bart Simpson T-shirt, bleeding from a fractured skull, Bouncy caught his breath.

Outdoor recess was cancelled. Bouncy got a four-day suspension.

The next year, when Grade Eight started, Bouncy was wearing hooded sweatshirts and voluminous pants. He had abandoned the mites, who now entertained themselves by throwing gourds in front of cars. Bouncy moved with Crustachio, a drug dealer with a velour-clad girlfriend and an extraordinary crustache that earned him his name. Bouncy rolled his belly as if he was Biggie, The Notorious B.I.G., and affected a ghetto limp, too big, too bad for bouncing.

✶

"Sup?"
"Not much, for shizzle."
"You be seeing my man, Crustachio?"
Bouncy slammed his locker door.
"No way, I fillin my time illin."
"Uh huh."
Bouncy rolled away from the locker, chin cocked like Marlon Brando doing Don Corleone. He passed an eighty-pound mite and slowly as if he was about to stroke a cat, reached out and slapped his head. Stung, the mite shook it off.
"You be doing home ec today?" Bouncy demanded.
"Ahh yeah."
"I wants all of yo cookies. Hear? Don't go hiding none."

✶

They called him Crustachio.

Before school each day, while kids were clustered like grapes, gossiping, fretting over hair, Crustachio stood on the curb with his girlfriend, kissing. Crustachio was sixteen, dressed in white fleece; his girlfriend was two years younger.

On cue, Crustachio would lift her into the air, feet off the ground, then back down. Faces pressed together, he would bend her over as if they were back in 1945 in Times Square, a jubilant sailor and a nurse, immortalized by Eisenstaedt as a symbol of VJ day joy and abandon. The show continued after school for twenty minutes until they parted, walking in opposite directions.

No one cared since Crustachio's eyes were decades old. He lived in a group home with two car thieves, a mentally challenged girl and a hood who punched a rival drug dealer in the face with a roll of quarters. His girlfriend was a skank.

One day, after an argument, the girlfriend avoided Crustachio. She brushed by with a preppy named Neil who lived in a brick two-storey with a BMW in the driveway. His mother stayed at home and his father was a lawyer. It was as though someone had unscrewed the light bulb in Crustachio's desolate room, unplugged the space heater.

In a funk, Crustachio started skipping school.

The school held a magic show in the auditorium. You needed a hall pass, earned with good attendance, to see The Sponge Ball Baffler and The Joker in the Deck. Crustachio would not be permitted to go, the principal announced over the PA system, using the teen's real name, Greg Lawlor. The mites convulsed at the absurdity of the reproof, at the thought of excluding the swarthy Crustachio from one hour of sleight of hand and deception.

While students yawned and teachers marvelled at a card trick involving an invisible string, Crustachio stared out a window.

✳

"Why you wearin dem tight pants, C?" jibed Gerry.

Gerry was a member of the junior G-Unit, which owned one corridor of the junior high, a hallway of wannabe gangstas and rap. Gerry worshipped 50 Cent, freestyle and all da shit from da ghetto.

Crustachio watched students leaving the high school next door. They passed through an honour guard of smokers, including a long-hair who looked like Weird Al. A chubby boy, who appeared thirty, ate a huge slab of pizza off a paper plate. A rich kid in braces jammed eight friends, all dressed by American Eagle and Gap, all laughing, into a Land Rover that glimmered like gold.

Gerry pointed at Crustachio's iPod and sneered, "Why you be listenin to that lollipop shit? Ja a bitch, man. You know that, doncha?"

"Holla at me when u got sumtin to say, Gerry."

"You goin soft, C, like Snoop?"

✳

That night, Bouncy and Crustachio stole a car.

A Cadillac Escalade SUV, the third choice of Canadian car thieves, behind the Ford 350 and the Subaru Impreza WRX. It was black.

It was later revealed that the Escalade belonged to the Chisholms, an ignominious family from the good part of town. The father owned slum dwellings with backed-up toilets and broken windows. The mother was a bully who harassed kids who refused to play with her loathsome offspring. She believed they were adorable and sent them to school in bizarre costumes, including sou'westers and fur hats. For weeks before Halloween, she released the eight-year-old onto the streets in a lime pimp suit, a fake fur coat and matching Mac Daddy hat, offending the sensibilities of everyone including the only blacks in the neighbourhood, a history professor and his wife.

Bouncy and Crustachio were unaware of the irony of the pimp suit and their random act of crime. That afternoon, they had taken ecstacy and gone to a tattoo parlour where they received matching bar codes on their calves.

Looking for something they could never find — peace, purpose, a future — they drove through town. They cruised Main Street past a massage parlour. As they passed a park, Crustachio slowed at the sight of a patrol car, then sped up again. In the rear-view mirror, he saw lights flash, on and off, as violently as a seizure. As he put his foot to the floor, Crustachio heard his mother's voice sobbing, "I tried everything I could. You *have* to believe me." He saw a man who may have been his father. He pressed harder. And then, the Escalade, the world's most powerful full-size SUV, lifted off just like Owen when he bounced through the air. Ooohhhhh! Bouncy took a swig from a two-litre Pepsi. They soared over a swamp of high rises until they landed in an open field of daisies. It was as though someone had filled the SUV with rocket fuel — liquid hydrogen and liquid oxygen — creating one stupendous thrust so powerful that it outran the cruel grip of destiny, the long arm of fate.

I am grateful to the following journals in which earlier versions of some of these stories first appeared: *Gaspereau Review*, *The Antigonish Review* and *Room of One's Own*. The title story, "The Watermelon Social," was also selected to appear in *The Journey Prize Stories 16*.

A Note on the Type

Galliard was designed by Matthew Carter (b. 1937) and issued by the Mergenthaler Printing Company for photocomposition in 1978. Its crisp and elegant mannerist letterforms are based on the roman and italic letters of the sixteenth-century French punch cutter, Robert Granjon (c. 1513–1590), arguably the greatest punchcutter who ever lived. The digital version used in this book was issued by Carter & Cone in 1997. At one time, type sizes were described using names, not numbers, and *Galliarde* was the French name for the nine-point size, which was called *Bourgeois* by the English and *Galjart* by the Dutch.

Text copyright © Elaine McCluskey, 2006
Illustration copyright © George Walker, 2006

All rights reserved. No part of this publication may be reproduced in any form without the prior written consent of the publisher. Any requests for the photocopying of any part of this book should be directed in writing to the Canadian Copyright Licensing Agency.

Gaspereau Press acknowledges the support of the Canada Council for the Arts, the Nova Scotia Department of Tourism, Culture & Heritage and the Government of Canada through the Book Publishing Industry Development Program.

Typeset in Galliard by Andrew Steeves & printed offset at Gaspereau Press.

7   6   5   4   3   2   1

Library and Archives Canada Cataloguing in Publication

McCluskey, Elaine, 1955–
   The watermelon social / Elaine McCluskey.

ISBN 1-55447-020-X
I. Title.
PS8625.C59W38 2006   C813'.6   C2005-907369-1

GASPEREAU PRESS LIMITED
Gary Dunfield & Andrew Steeves Printers & Publishers
47 Church Avenue, Kentville, Nova Scotia
Canada B4N 2M7   www.gaspereau.com